C. K. Stead

THE SECRET HISTORY OF MODERNISM

V

VINTAGE

Published by Vintage 2003

2 4 6 8 10 9 7 5 3 1

First published in Great Britain in 2001 by
The Harvill Press

Vintage
Random House, 20 Vauxhall Bridge Road,
London SW1V 2SA

Random House Australia (Pty) Limited
20 Alfred Street, Milsons Point, Sydney
New South Wales 2061, Australia

Random House New Zealand Limited
18 Poland Road, Glenfield,
Auckland 10, New Zealand

Random House (Pty) Limited
Endulini, 5A Jubilee Road, Parktown 2193,
South Africa

The Random House Group Limited Reg. No. 954009
www.randomhouse.co.uk

A CIP catalogue record for this book
is available from the British Library

ISBN 0 09 944706 1

Papers used by Random House are natural, recyclable products
made from wood grown in sustainable forests. The manufactur-
ing processes conform to the environmental regulations of the
country of origin

Printed and bound in Great Britain by
Bookmarque Ltd, Croydon, Surrey

SPECIAL THANKS TO GERRARD FRIEDLANDER
IN AUCKLAND
AND EVA (ROSENBAUM) REID
IN MELBOURNE

ONE

Hitler's Nose

MY NAME IS LASZLO WINTER. I'M A NOVELIST, AND FOR the purposes of this identification we will begin in Auckland, New Zealand, at the beginning of the new century, a time when I'd been experiencing, for perhaps three months, perhaps six, something new for me, an obstacle commonly called writer's block. Maybe my writing life was over. Maybe it, and I, belonged to the old century, and could be rounded off with a retrospect, some sort of autobiography – or "memoir" as some of my similarly-placed writing colleagues (Dick Flinders notably – and we will come to him) had lately been calling their books of recollection, a description used, I'd begun to think, as an excuse for invention, inaccuracy, and the settling of old scores.

Or perhaps I might let myself off writing altogether, and simply close up for ever the room in the back garden where my work has been done, the structure I refer to mostly as "the shed" (humbler than it deserves), but also as "the studio" (pretentious), "the office" (too businesslike), and "the Lockwood" (name of its manufacturer).

Sometimes I thought of joining a gym, losing the weight gained, and regaining the muscle lost, in the past ten or fifteen years. Sometimes of buying a piece of cheap land and building a kitset house (a Lockwood, perhaps). Then there was the thought of slugging my way through all the unread books I knew I ought to have read, and still wanted to read. Or of giving in entirely to my passive addiction to movies. Or of travelling all over New Zealand on a bicycle. Or of accepting Louise's idea (Louise is my wife, and French) that we should sell everything and decamp to eat and drink ourselves to death in the French countryside . . .

But at the same time that I thought up these schemes for a new life I was listless, lacking the purpose and energy necessary to make them more than whimsical dreams. I was always picking up a newspaper or magazine, which was really an excuse to lie down. When I lay down to read, I slept. When I woke I was tired. I knew (or thought I knew) I wasn't ill. It was, I supposed, a mild depression. I felt healthy, discontented, exhausted.

Any of these plans of action might, if there were ever an objective measure of better and worse, be better than telling yet another story, or another (as mine tended to be) story within-a-story within-a . . . (and so on), my narrative habits tending to the structural character of a Russian doll. But there is something about stories which compel those who write them and those who read or listen to them. Shakespeare's Richard II, as power slips away from him and as the forces that will destroy him close in, says:

> "For God's sake let us sit upon the ground
> And tell sad stories of the death of Kings . . . "

And doesn't he instruct his wife, anticipating the time when he will be dead, "Tell thou the lamentable tale of me"? But then most of Shakespeare's doomed or dying kings and tragic heroes find an occasion to issue instructions about how their lives are to be recorded. They long for the structure of narrative, so that death will not be meaningless and random, but the rounding off of a story – a sad one, they hope, so if in the end they have not love, at least they will have pity. Othello says:

> " . . . then you must speak
> Of one that lov'd not wisely but too well"

– a line that should be stored up by every potential wife strangler for the moment when the corpse lies limp and the sirens are getting nearer. Best, of course, is Hamlet's:

> "Absent thee from felicity awhile,
> And in this harsh world draw thy breath in pain
> To tell my story."

Long ago my son, then aged I suppose about ten and set the task of reading a story to his younger sister, cut the reading short, when he grew tired of the chore, with the sentence, "And then Laura died," producing a wail of grief and protest. In fact the book, or series of books, he was reading from, never reached Laura's death, but there's a sense in which he was cutting straight through to the inevitable. Even kings must die, as Shakespeare's Richard, with his longing for narrative, comes to recognize, and so would Laura Ingalls Wilder.

When, at this time I'm speaking about, I cast my eyes over the books I had written, I began to notice that if they had a single subject it was the century just ended. They appeared to be about many different things, but were really about just one: the fifty years of human history I had lived through with an adult consciousness, and how the earlier fifty, which I knew by reading and report, bore upon them. Perhaps that (I began

3

to think) explained my writer's block. My time was up. The story I'd made it my business to tell had come to an end, not quite with a whimper, but only with the bangs of the millennial fireworks.

But that was no more than an excuse, even if, momentarily, a compelling one. That we counted our years from the supposed birth-date of the supposed Son of a supposed God, and that we called one year 1999 and the next 2000 (I'm attempting to reconstruct my laboured thoughts of that time), was no more than a convention, a convenience. To the cells of my body, as to the cat sleeping in the garden, and the thrush pecking scraps from his dish (the cat was suffering from hunter's block), these identifications meant nothing at all. Nothing had ended. Life was going on. Human history had not checked itself in its stride, and then made a new start as the fireworks subsided – and if, from another point of view, it had, what did that signify? It might be a reason for telling the century's "lamentable tale" once again, since now it truly had arrived at its ending. Either way, it seemed, I had no excuse. The shed/studio/office/Lockwood was out there still, and the calendar could not be construed as an obstacle.

And stories were necessary, not just to me, but to everyone. Over time the popular medium might have changed for most of the human race – from oral to the written word, from the written word to the movie and television screen; but the need remained. Without stories everything flew apart and became shapeless, nameless, meaningless; and the more we learned about ourselves and our place in the dreadful exploding-and-dying universe we now know we inhabit, the more essential they became. Stories were the saviours of our sanity.

With thoughts of this kind I (as we say these days) "psyched

4

myself up". I would not build a house, or cycle down the two long islands of my homeland, or lift weights, or spend my twilight in the other twilight of movie houses; I would not even do *la belle France* the honour of bequeathing her my bones. I would go back to work.

All very well. A fine resolution. A ringing (though inward) declaration of intent. But what was I to write about? Where was my "story"?

At about this time I had a phone call. A voice identified itself, in a German accent, as Otto Stiltz, and asked whether that name "rang any bells" for me. It did, just one bell, and by such a large coincidence that I, looking for omens, seized upon it. That very day, searching for something in my battered and crammed little address book, held together by a broad rubber band and listing a not insignificant number beside whose names there is now a large D, my eye had lit on just that name. What caught my attention was that it and the address, a town or village in the Langue d'Oc, were written in square, almost-print writing that was not my own. Beside the address, in the same square letters, explaining the general location (otherwise indicated only by the postal code), the person had added, "NEAR P. du G."; and off to the side of this went a spidery arrow, and in my own writing the words "Pont du Gard", evidently added so I would later know what "P. du G." stood for.

Further, although I remembered nothing about Otto Stiltz, and could not recall even his face, I did remember the circumstance in which he had written his name and address in my book; and because I remembered that much, I was able to be certain of the date. It was November 1980. I flew from Nice to Munich where I was to stay with an old friend, a scientist then working at the Max Planck Institute, after which I was to travel on by rail to the ancient city of Regensburg where I would eat sausage and sauerkraut, drink Thurn und Taxis ale, and read from my work in a vault-ceilinged cellar applauded by the banging of Bavarian fists and tankards on heavy wooden table-tops. As my plane came in to land I saw that snow was falling, the first (and early) snow of the winter season, which seemed all the more dramatic to one who had come direct from the mildness of the Côte d'Azur.

My friend was waiting for me beyond the Customs barrier, and his face was grim. News had just come through that Ronald Reagan had defeated Jimmy Carter and would be the next President of the United States.

I was at once as depressed as my friend. Reagan had presented himself as such a rocket-rattler, so simple-and single-minded in his wish to lock horns with what he called (Hollywood-style) "the Evil Empire", we both, my friend and I, thought the world would now be stepping back into the worst danger-times of the Cold War. Once again we would have reason to fear a nuclear exchange, a prospect which had seemed to recede under the benign and fuzzy presidency of peanut farmer Jimmy Carter.

Well, we were wrong. President Ronnie was to be, or to become, as benign and fuzzy as President Jimmy. The next eight years of Soviet-American affairs would be, not all bullying and bluster, threat and counter-threat, but as if the Alzheimer's Disease that would eventually lead Ronnie off into the shadows was already causing him to forget the enemy's name. The *Soviets* (in his husky, confiding, almost-whisper)? Those nice big bears in furry hats? Surely not!

But it was the feeling of anxiety, almost of fear, at the

6

news of the Reagan triumph, which impressed itself on my memory — that together with the unexpectedly early fall of snow, which seemed to take on symbolic significance. And now, as my friend went to get his car and I waited with my luggage, a person I didn't recognize came up and introduced himself.

So many years later I no longer remembered his face, or his connection with me; and I know now that he hadn't explained the connection because he'd taken for granted that I would know it. All I'd registered (still, I suppose, thinking about Ronald Reagan, and reluctant to talk to a stranger) was that this person seemed to know me and was keen to give me his address so if I should ever visit his part of France I would know there was someone to offer me shelter and to make me welcome.

He had written his name and address in my book; I had added the words "Pont du Gard" to explain his "NEAR P.du G"; he had gone on his way; and I had forgotten him until this afternoon when my eye lit on the entry. And now here he was on the phone, inviting me for a drink at what he called "the sherry hour", though he assured me he would not offer sherry unless I especially wanted it. Of course, he added, my wife/partner was also invited, if I had one.

I confirmed that I had: Louise.

"Louise," he repeated. "So it's not . . . " and he stopped. Once again I was puzzled by the impression he gave of knowing me well.

I asked, "Which name were you expecting?"

"Euro . . . Evro . . . It was a Greek name, was it?"

"Evrodiki," I said, trying to sound amused but not, I suppose, quite concealing an irritable embarrassment. I had

had a number of wives. (The number was three.) "She was my first."

"Well, Laszlo and Louise," he said. "They go very well together."

"The names do, yes," I agreed.

"And the couple too, I'm sure."

"I hope so," I said, revealing to myself, as well as to him, an uncertainty. There was a brief reflective silence. When I couldn't write, nothing seemed safe, nothing certain.

"So," I said. "A drink. When?"

He said it was for me to choose day and time. He had only recently arrived and had no present engagements in Auckland. He knew I was a busy man, but if I could spare him an hour or two . . .

It was the sort of phone call I might at a busier moment have considered an invasion. But that was not what I felt. Consciously or not, I was still casting about for a story – a light for my darkness, a flame for my fuse. Anything might do. These things were always unpredictable. One had to be open – to the world, to suggestion. One had meekly to hold out one's cloth cap and hope Chance would drop a coin in it. And then, when the illumination was found, the fuse lit, the coin lying there, one could close all doors and get on with it.

Otto Stiltz had come into some family money and had bought himself a pied-à-terre apartment on the 21st floor of a new high-rise block in central Auckland. He would still spend most of his year in the northern hemisphere. But three months of the northern winter, which was quite severe in the part of France he'd made his home, he intended to enjoy Auckland's summer, high up overlooking the Harbour where, not long before, Team New Zealand's *Black Magic*, and Italy's

Luna Rossa, had been seen each day towed out into the Hauraki Gulf to race for the America's Cup, preceded and followed by thousands of spectator craft of every size from jet skis, one-paddler canoes, and dinghies up to large ferries and even a cruise liner: one wide and seemingly endless trail of boats streaming out from beaches and marinas, churning the calm blue waters into a white turbulence, like a re-enactment of Dunkirk.

In fact it had been the America's Cup Challenger Series, shown on French television in the early stages because there had been a French boat among the dozen or so contenders, and then because the Italians had defeated the Americans for the right (as it turned out) to be beaten five-nil by New Zealand, that had made Otto choose Auckland as the place to spend his southern summers. The challenge races had been much closer and more exciting than those of the final. They'd been sailed in higher winds and rougher seas, with injuries, protests, hysterical helmsmen, near and actual collisions, split spinnakers and torn sails, a broken mast, even a boat cracked amidships and bent upward at either end like a banana, the crew diving overboard as it threatened to sink. Otto had watched night after night, captured by the drama of it, and the beauty. The Gulf with its islands, especially Rangitoto, had looked, he said, such a fine natural setting, and Auckland in the background such a beautiful city.

"And already, Laszlo," he told me, "I had an image of the place in my mind, taken from your books. These television pictures – they confirmed it."

He offered us "a Chardonnay, a pinot noir, or Moët". I hesitated over the pinot noir, but followed Louise in choosing the champagne. He put out good bread in neat slices, some with liver paté, some with a nice pale cheese; and on another dish some little German shortbread cakes that were unusual in being salty rather than sweet. We drank one another's health. He told me that he'd been in A when Evrodiki and I had been in B; and that at the very time we moved to B, he had moved to C, so we had failed to meet. He had even bought a ticket to hear me read at a literary festival somewhere in the world and missed it because of some breakdown or lateness of bus or train or plane. But he had read all my books, had opinions about them and a clear order of preference – a Germanic thoroughness I found pleasing and also faintly intimidating.

Still pretending that I knew him as well as he supposed I did, I mentioned our encounter at Munich airport but strangely this, the only thing I remembered about him, he had entirely forgotten.

And then, when I felt myself floundering on the brink of explaining to him that, regrettably, I couldn't recall what the link between us was, and didn't know why he seemed to feel I should, he asked (with a discreet cough, as if to say he hoped the question was not out of place) whether Sammy and I still kept in touch.

Sammy! I'd only ever known one person of that name.

"Ah yes," I said, casual, trying not to behave as if a darkness had suddenly been illuminated. "We sometimes get a card at Christmas. I'm not very good about such things. Is she well?"

He gave me what news he had of her.

"Sammy was lovely," I said, and meant it.

"She was." And then after a moment, "She was the great love of my life. I was only a minor mistake in hers."

I couldn't think how to respond to that; and really, no

response was necessary. He spoke without bitterness. "Minor," he added, "and quickly corrected. It was never going to work. She was on the rebound from a rebound when I met her."

Now I had my bearings.

During my years in London as a post-graduate student Samantha Conlan –Sammy – had been a friend; a very good, a dear friend; but those were also the years of her great love affair with Freddy Goldstein.

Later, when her affair with Freddy was over, I heard she had returned home to Sydney where she had married a university lecturer, a German; and then, within a year or eighteen months, that she'd divorced him. She wrote a card telling me of the divorce, saying, "It was no use. I don't know what I thought I was doing. I feel very guilty. I treated him very badly, poor man."

Otto Stiltz, on the other hand, must have heard about me direct from Sammy, which would explain why he had been such a conscientious reader of my books. If, as he said, she had been "the great love of his life", he would have been, and probably remained, fascinated by everything about her, including friends she talked about whom he had never met.

So why, I asked, if he wanted to come back to this part of the world, had he not returned to Sydney? "Two reasons," he said at once. "Bad memories on that side of the Tasman, and a weaker dollar on this. And besides, I wanted a new place, new experience." He hesitated, and then, "No going back," he said, giving it special emphasis. It was the title of one of my novels.

Now our conversation, which had tripped and stumbled, took off. Questions, answers, reminiscence, reflection. We were, Otto and I, of an age. We lived for, and by, the printed word – he the scholar, I the writer. We had homes, children, roots of a kind. But we were also, or had become over the years, sky-riders, continent-crossers, citizens, if not quite of the world, at least of the world of the 747-400 and economy-class travel.

We had also been political liberals through the Cold War which had seemed destined either to go on for ever or (more likely) to end in disaster, and had seen it end as if by something as inevitable and welcome as the arrival of a late spring. The days had grown longer, the sun had climbed higher in the sky, and the long terrifying winter was over. Or (to abandon metaphor for what my dad would have called 'the fact of the matter') the Soviet Union had run out of cash and credit and, as if to prove, even at its own expense, that Marx had been right when he argued that everything significant in human history was determined by economics, *down* had come the Berlin Wall, and with it the Party that had ruled in his name.

We talked about Suez and Hungary; about the Cuban Missile Crisis, the death of Kennedy, Vietnam. Two hours went by. The champagne was gone, the plates empty, and it seemed we were only getting started. Clearly we would have to meet again.

Otto Stiltz was slow spoken, cautiously intelligent. Once or twice, before we were swept away by political history, he mentioned trusts and inheritances. He came (or that was my impression) from a solid burgher family. After his divorce from Sammy he had married again, a French woman (we had this in common). There had been children, and another divorce, after which he'd opted out of university teaching to live, still in France, the life of a solo bookish gentleman, a scholar whose researches were now for the edification of no one but himself.

Sammy had written something else on that long-ago post-card – something which now came back to me. She'd filled the message-half of the card, right to the bottom. Then up the side she'd added in her smallest, neatest hand, "Rumpelstilt-skin with Hitler's nose – what was I thinking of? *Mad*!"

This was typical of Sammy. On paper, and even in conversation, she was often cryptic. It was partly because she tended to assume that if she knew something, you must know it too, so it didn't need elaboration. But it was also her style. If she had to choose between making an impression, and being understood, she preferred to make an impression.

Who, then, was this "Rumpelstiltskin"? He was the dwarf in the Grimm Brothers' fairy story who spun straw into gold – that much I knew. I'd puzzled over what she might mean, which was why I remembered it – and now at last it made sense. Sammy, who liked to play with people's names, would have assumed that I knew her husband's, and that I would recognize it in "Rumpelstiltskin". But further, now that I had him sitting opposite me in the same room, I could make sense of the rest of what she had written. Otto Stiltz's nose was very straight and pointed. It was, to a T, the nose of Adolf Hitler.

A child of that time, I had always thought of Hitler's cartoon moustache, his cartoon lock of hair brushed forward over the brow, his mad bulgy cartoon eyes. I'd never thought about the nose until, prompted by the memory of Sammy's postscript, I recognized it now on Otto Stiltz.

Only a few days before I'd watched a programme about the Second World War: Hitler strutting and shouting and snatching with one hand at the air in front of his face, as if menaced by poisonous flies. Forests of raised arms and choruses of "Heil!". Tanks rolling, skies full of droning wings, bombs falling, buildings collapsing, cities burning. Then the dead and the walking dead at the war's end when the camps were opened, the piles of corpses, the gas chambers and crematoria.

It was a part of one's growing up, all that, and an unfailing horror and disbelief went with it. And this programme included new film (or new to me) of the Warsaw ghetto – children hungry and in rags, dying in the streets. And a close-up of a child's face, curiously misshapen, infinitely touching, with just the faint beginnings of a smile as he looks into the camera lens of the liberators of Buchenwald.

It was not Stiltskin's fault that he had Schiklgruber's nose; nor was this new acquaintance of mine of an age to have even the remotest responsibility for what had been done in those terrible years. It was just (in a very precise sense) a *co*-incidence – Hitler, the Jews, Sammy's Jewish boyfriend Friedrich Goldstein, and finally Sammy's postscript making sense at last: "What was I thinking of? *Mad!*"

To protect myself in case this voice on the phone, this unknown Otto Stiltz, should prove uncongenial, I had invented a dinner invitation for 7.30. In fact Louise and I had booked a table at a restaurant in Mission Bay. Now I thought of inviting him to join us there, but couldn't quite bring myself to confess a lie which would in turn have revealed how much less I'd known of him than he supposed.

We were parked in Princes Street, outside the university. Otto came down in the lift and walked with us up through Albert Park, to see us off. We shook hands warmly and promised to meet again.

It was a calm summer evening and Louise and I sat out on the terrace of the restaurant, looking on to a street noisy enough to be somewhere in Italy, and over a sea blue enough in the evening light to be the Mediterranean. The restaurant's owner and cook, Barry, we'd known for some years. His partner, Donny, a shy kindly old queen in a startlingly embossed t-shirt, played the piano without sheet music and with appalling fluency, surrounded by bric-à-brac (statuettes, a marble bust, a Satsuma vase, plastic flowers, Art Nouveau glassware), at least one item of which was said to have belonged to (of course) Oscar Wilde.

"It Had to Be You", "Unforgettable", "Moon River", "Some Day I'll Find You", "Stardust", "The Man I Love", "Lily Marlene", "Blue Moon", "Autumn Leaves", "I'm in the Mood for Love", "My Heart Belongs to Daddy" – one popular favourite of the past half century drifted into another, on and on, so you were several bars into the new "number" before you recognized that the previous one was over. It was like the ear-equivalent (in slow motion) of the whole of life flashing before your eyes. In his own way, and without aspiring to be, Donny was a social historian. He was also one of what my son (a musician as well as the killer of Laura Ingalls Wilder) used to call "easy listening criminals". But the sounds were soothing – because they were written to be, and because they were familiar, and because when you are called back far enough into your own past even the bad times and the bad taste can arouse nostalgia.

We ordered our courses, enjoyed them and the wine, watched the crowd, talked about the past, mine long gone, Louise's more recent. Afterwards we walked along the beach holding hands. It was too hot for hand-holding but Louise required it. Being French, she liked always to create *une belle image*.

We looked at the people, Pakeha and Maori, Asian and Polynesian, promenading, talking, sitting on the grass and the sea-wall, eating takeaways, playing guitars and singing. Beyond the beach, on the town side, the pohutukawa-topped cliffs were flood-lit; across the water, the dark shape of Rangitoto loomed; and between, the moon made its white-footed way over a summer-night sea. I was happy. I loved it all, and I loved Louise. This was my comfort zone. I didn't want to break out of it; but the thought was there somewhere that I might have to if there was ever to be another book.

Why should there be another? Why not settle now for silence and anonymity? No more bruising public attention. No more wounding reviews. But it was too late for that. Already something new — a hint, an inkling — was stirring. "Samantha Conlan". "Sammy". There can be magic in a name. A name can conjure up a world, and "a world" can be a story. It wasn't just that I thought, wearily as with other recent ideas, that, well, it might be worth a shot. It was that I wanted to do it. I was alert, awake, seeing colours, hearing sounds.

When we got home I was too restless for bed. I tried to read, toyed with the TV remote, looked over the rejected drafts of what I'd thought might be a novel and rejected them again, this time emphatically, screwing them up and throwing them into the basket.

On my laptop there was a letterhead with name, address, phone and fax numbers, and email. I'd concocted it recently under Microsoft instructions, didn't like it, and now couldn't discover how to remove it. Under it I wrote:

16

Dear Sammy,

I will send this to the last address of yours I have – no doubt out of date, but maybe someone there will remember you (as I do fondly) and send it on.

A visitor to Auckland has stirred ancient memories. Frankly, I'm of a mind to stir them further. Are you? Do you have email? Should we exchange?

Ever your friend,

Laszlo

I'd noticed lately a tendency (part of my depression) to begin things and then to doubt, to dither, not "follow through". At this moment the wine was still in charge. In the morning everything might look different. And perhaps Louise would not encourage this shot in the dark. I found an envelope and stamp for my note and went out at once into the night to post it.

A week or ten days later there was an email reply:

Laszlo:

Yes I do, and yes I am. Speak, Memory!

Sammy.

Speak, Memory! Nabokov, of course. With Sammy there was always a book, or a book reference. Now when my memory failed me, hers might come to its aid.

TWO

T. S. Eliot's Rose Garden

SCENES ARE IMPORTANT. LIFE, MORE LIKE A VERY LONG novel than "a dome of many-coloured glass", falls into discrete but interlocking narratives, and narratives break into scenes. That's how we hold on to "what happens", how we process it, extracting and ordering the essentials and ridding ourselves of the copiousness of impression and sensation. Memory, if we didn't contain it, would destroy us. So everything must be simplified, and in that sense falsified.

Scenes then. Here is just one:

It is 11 or 12 January, 1957 and I am coming out into Malet Street from London University's Senate House Library. Ahead of me, between the wrought iron gates, I see two of my friends, the young Australian woman, Sammy Conlan, and the Delhi Brahman, Rajiv Battacharya. Rajiv (he has taught us to pronounce it Rajiu) is astride his bicycle, metal clips holding in the bottoms of his trousers so they won't flap against the grease of the chain. He is waving a newspaper, and I can see he's distressed. His voice is raised, there are even tears in his always bloodshot eyes, and he's saying, "Bloody hell, Sammy. This man has deceived us."

For a moment I pause to take in the scene, not just because of the little drama Rajiv is creating, but because I'm struck all over again by beautiful Samantha – olive-skinned, hazel-eyed, thick black hair tied back in a pony-tail, her brown jacket and matching skirt good, stylish, fashionable (which in the 1950s means rather formal), not inexpensive (Sammy is from an affluent family) but not ostentatious either.

She's smiling, not much troubled by whatever it is that has upset our Indian friend, and as I approach now she takes the *Evening Standard* out of his hand and holds it towards me. "Laszlo," she says, "have you seen this?"

I look at the headline. It reads, T. S. ELIOT, AND HOW THE LOVE GREW YOUNGER THAN SPRINGTIME.

I cast my eyes over the item, written in gossip-columnese. The great American-born, English-naturalised poet T. S. Eliot, it informs his fellow-Londoners, winner of the Nobel Prize for Literature, the Order of Merit, "and other awards too numerous to mention," now aged sixty-eight, has secretly married his secretary, Valerie Fletcher, aged thirty. The story goes on to tell how long and slow their courtship has been; how his secretary has always called him Mr Eliot and he has called her Miss Fletcher; how the love each has hidden from the other blossomed first when they found themselves together, "by chance", in the Mediterranean town of Menton . . .

I read quickly, skipping and skimming. There's a photograph of the "newly-weds", he in his "four-piece suit" (as Virginia Woolf once mocked) and overcoat, carrying homburg and walking stick and looking shy and distinguished; she, "frightfully English", young, in an open fur coat, wearing a necklace of three solid strands and a small hat like a punctuation mark, a circumflex over the round O of her face. She's looking very happy and satisfied. He looks happy too, but as if happiness, which had been no part of his long-term plan, has taken him by surprise and is causing him some embarrassment.

So the old bastard has rejoined the human race! I look up from the paper. Sammy and I smile at one another. Then we both look at Rajiv. Those are real tears. The dim light of a London winter shines on them. I say, "Come on Rajiv. This is good news."

He shakes his head and looks away up the street where a few flakes of what might be the beginnings of a sleet shower swirl about in a sudden updraught. Quietly but with a low, wailing intensity, the question addressed more to himself than to us, he asks, "Vere is his rose garden now, for goodness sake."

I will explain those tears. But first . . .

Sammy, Rajiv and I had arrived in London six months before on the P&O liner, the *Orsova*, where we'd first met and where, during the long boring engine-throbbing food-smelling days, we'd become friends. I had boarded the ship in Auckland, Sammy in Sydney, Rajiv in Bombay. We were university graduates in our early twenties, Rajiv and I intending to do post-graduate work in English – I on a scholarship, Rajiv on money provided by his family of Delhi lawyers and civil servants. Sammy had a good Honours B.A. from Sydney but she had no interest in further formal education. She came with a modest allowance from her mother – enough to live on for a year or two – and wanted, she said, "time, space and distance" in which to sort out her life.

My subject of study hadn't been exactly settled, but it was going to be something in the area of Shakespeare and Jacobean

Drama. Rajiv had come so well-prepared that his thesis had a name even before the work was begun. It was to be called "T. S. Eliot and the Pursuit of the Divine."

Sammy was passionate about poetry in general, and modern poetry in particular. She knew it as a jockey knows horses – close up. She went to poetry readings, read literary magazines, picked up literary gossip through the pores of her skin. So she had more interest in Rajiv's work than in mine; and in the months since we'd arrived in London she had become, almost, his research assistant.

It happened first by chance. Rajiv was complaining that he would have to take time off to hunt out something published by T. S. Eliot long ago in a literary periodical and never reprinted. Journals of that early period weren't kept at the British Museum, where he was working every day in the Reading Room, but in an annex out at Colindale on the Northern Line. Sammy offered to go out there and do the search for him. She was successful – found and copied what he wanted; and a week or so later went out there again to hunt for something else.

Soon Rajiv had got her a British Museum reader's ticket and she was there every day, sometimes helping him, often working on her own at something she began to call her *Secret History of Modernism*, which she said would be neither a work of literary criticism nor a work of fiction, but somewhere in between. She was doing it to please herself, not believing it would ever be published, and not caring about that, but becoming more and more absorbed in it. Sometimes she let me read chapters or parts of chapters. I still have two or three faded and blurred fourth-carbon quarto copies (these were pre-xerox days) of extracts that were really interlocking stories from the lives of twentieth-century writers, taken from biographies, memoirs, newspaper and journal interviews, published letters; and sometimes, after Sammy discovered the British Museum Manuscript Room, direct from unpublished sources.

She was living with a group of young Australian and New Zealand women in a big flat in Castlenau Mansions, just south of the river over the Hammersmith Bridge. She'd come to London knowing her friends had a space reserved for her there, but she'd brought Rajiv and me as well, straight from Tilbury where the *Orsova* docked, and for a week or so we'd been allowed to doss down on the sitting room floor until we found ourselves places to live.

At first Rajiv and I had thought we might share a small flat, but in those days his colour was an obstacle. Twice I answered an advertisement and seemed on the brink of securing a place for us, and then the offer became vague, "to be confirmed later", when I mentioned that the friend I was to share with was Indian.

"I have to be so careful these days, Luv," a landlady with rouged cheeks and mauve hair explained to me, looking around her dark damp basement flat.

"Careful." I repeated it carefully.

"Colour's creeping in," she said, with a sideways movement of the head.

I stared at her. "On the buses," she explained, in a sort of whisper, as if the air was being sucked out of her. She meant the West Indians just then being recruited to work for London Transport.

I explained that my friend was from India, not Trinidad, and then felt guilty, as if I'd acknowledged that it wouldn't be unreasonable to object to a West Indian. But she was shaking her head in a helpless way, murmuring "No, I . . . I'm afraid . . ."

I could see it didn't matter whether he was Indian, West Indian, Red Indian. There was some obscure force, beyond her powers to prevent, ruling that whatever he might be, "Colour" would not cross her threshold.

We'd climbed the stairs up to street level. At the door I said, "Well anyway, it wouldn't have done. My friend's fastidious."

It was meant to be cutting, to put her in her place, but "fastidious" was beyond her. She smiled saying goodbye, and even wished me luck. Perhaps she thought "fastidious" was my brown friend's religion.

And then, going together to an address where a local newsagent had told me there was a flat to let, Rajiv and I were met at the front door by an ill-written sign stuck inside the glass panel:

VACANCY
(No Irish, No Colurds)

It was one of those half houses, of which there were still a lot to be seen, its other half destroyed in the bombing, and the wall, that had once divided the two, supported by beams sloping up from what was left of the basement on the bombed-out side. There used to be feral cats in those open basements, living among broken stones and the kind of plant life – buddleia and bracken – that might return after London was nuked in the final East–West shoot-out we all feared and half expected.

"It's no good," Rajiv said as we walked back into the street and stood, momentarily at a loss among the smelly litter spilling from bins. He was philosophical about it. "It's not important. It doesn't matter." And it was really as if it didn't; as if he accepted that the world was full of things which, for your own protection, you had simply not to notice.

He told me he had addresses, Indian friends of friends. They would help him. A few days later he'd found a place with a family somewhere in Islington, from where he could ride his bicycle to University College and the British Museum. For myself, I found a bed-sit in Kensington.

Kensington sounds very grand but it wasn't. It cost me £2.17/6 a week – gas by shilling in the meter; lavatory shared with two other bed-sits, and bathroom shared with those two and with the downstairs flat occupied by a fish-delivery man whose name, Harry Pulsford, Sammy converted to How Repulsive. "Hullo Mr Pulsive," she said, passing him on the stairs on her way to visit me.

"Pulsford," he called after her. "And please call me 'Arry."

Harry Pulsford, who seemed to be the landlady's boyfriend, grew fishier each day of the week until Sunday morning when, cleanliness and godliness coming together, he locked himself for an hour or more in that shared bathroom, where the hissing shuddering gas geyser seemed always on the point of exploding, and sweated and soaped himself back to neutral.

Of the two bed-sits, one was occupied by Heather, a slim Bristol girl with wavy chestnut hair whose face lit up like a lantern when she smiled; the other by Mr Spiteri from Malta. Mr Spiteri went to and from work at office hours, but Heather's day was irregular. When the phone on the landing (another facility shared by the three bed-sits) rang for her it was always a woman with a baritone voice who would say, "Is Heather there? Tell her it's the *shop*." Then one day Heather spilled her handbag on the stairs, and when she'd gathered it all together and gone out, I found a card that had flipped through the bannisters lying on the carpet below. It had a generalized sketch of a buxom girl. "Miss Tina of AWAYCARE promises to see to your every need in London", it said, and there was a telephone number that must have been "the shop". Heather (I later confirmed) was a call girl, taken out to suppers and dances by businessmen visiting the city, and then back to the visitor's hotel where she saw to their every need.

Although Mr Spiteri was so regular I heard rather than saw him, and wouldn't have found it easy to pick him out of a line-up. Now and then we would pass on the stairs, he galloping up or down, a compact young man in a shiny dark suit, shiny dark hair, and a waft of hair oil. I assumed he was from Malta because that was where his mail came from; and I knew his name because he had it pinned to his door on a card:

"MR. SPITERI"

The double inverted commas, Sammy and I thought, suggested that he, or the name, or both, were unreal. One evening, when she called for me on the way to a play or concert, she brought a new notice on a new piece of card. It appeared to be just the same as the original until you looked closely and saw that it read,

"MR. SPITFIRE"

There was no light under his door. She took down the old card and replaced it. In the days that followed I looked for some reaction – a correction to the card at least, but there was none. Either he didn't notice or he didn't mind, because that's how it remained.

But although I saw so little of my nearest neighbour, I used to hear him every morning, through the wall, using the shared lavatory which he was always in too much of a hurry to flush, no matter what he'd left in it. He never bothered with toilet paper either. In there "MR. SPITFIRE" became "MR. LANCASTER BOMBER" – a big loud no-nonsense shitter, very healthy I would guess, eating a diet that included plenty of oils, fruit, red beans and green vegetables.

Sammy at that time was deeply in love with Friedrich Goldstein, a journalist who had gone from Auckland to work in Sydney where they'd met and been lovers. Freddy (as she called him) had given six month's notice on the paper he worked for, the *Sydney Morning Herald*, and would soon be coming to London. That was why Sam had come. "I didn't want to seem to be chasing him," she'd told me one night, as we stood at the rail of the ship, swishing through the hot dead waters of the Red Sea.

She'd read a book (with Sammy, as I've said, there was always a book) by Christina Stead called *For Love Alone*, in which a young Sydney woman had gone to London in pursuit of the man she'd fallen in love with. Sam didn't want to see herself in that role. "So I came first," she said. "This way, he'll be chasing me."

But she knew Friedrich Goldstein wasn't, and wouldn't be, chasing her. He was a married man; and it occurred to me, and probably to her, that his plan to leave Sydney and look for work in London might have been in order to escape from her. Or perhaps I should say to escape from his emotional entanglement with her, his Sammy- addiction, because if what she told me was true, their affair in Sydney had run red-hot Friedrich was yet to arrive, and in the meantime Sammy, courageous, redoubtable, but full of half-repressed anxieties, liked to talk about him, keeping him right there in the fore-front of her thoughts, not letting all this new experience that London represented diminish his importance.

But I said I would explain Rajiv's tears. This will require (if you will forgive me) a short disquisition on the subject of T. S. Eliot.

We were, Samantha Conlan, Rajiv Battacharya, and Laszlo Winter, all in our different ways, interested (I use a neutral word, but with my two friends it veered towards obsession) in Eliot. He was not just the great poet of the age. He was also a playwright, successful in the West End and on Broadway. He was the major twentieth-century literary critic, so totally dominant that in universities it seemed no one could write, or even lecture, on any major figure or move-ment in the history of literature in English without making at least passing (and often more than passing) mention of what he'd said on the subject. Finally he was poetry editor of Faber and Faber, whose list he lent credibility and status simply by his presence and his name. To be published by Faber put you into the first rank of poets, whether or not your work deserved it.

Eliot was a strange mix – literary revolutionary, political and social reactionary. Like Picasso in painting and Stravinsky in music, he was famous for works which excited people who considered themselves "avant garde", and enraged the ones who liked to assert that they didn't know anything about painting/music/poetry but "knew what they liked". Eliot was also a very public Anglo-Catholic convert who wrote Christian plays and poems which Christians found obscure and disappointing, while non-believers professed to understand and admire them. His political views were declared in sentences so round-about and back-to-front they gave no comfort to the old bulldog Tories they ought to have pleased, while young Leftists read and wrestled with them, deplored and excused them, because their author was the great poet of the age and an editor they terribly hoped to impress.

Eliot was public property. Journalists would ask him what his latest play *meant*, and express puzzlement, exasperation, even rage (though of course it was just what they wanted) when he lived up to expectation and replied, "It means what you want it to mean."

Sam's interest in Eliot was almost as obsessive as Rajiv's. And although he was of less interest to me, he figured in my work as well, because my subject was the English drama of the early 1600s, and Eliot had had something to say about every one of the major playwrights of that time. There was no way around him. I had to take on board what he'd written on my topic, understand it, and deal with it.

Before the news of his late second marriage broke, there had been an on-going disagreement between Sammy and Rajiv about Eliot's poetry, an argument in which I tried (and failed) to fill the role of peacemaker. Sammy believed Eliot had written his best poems long ago. For her, *The Waste Land*, published in 1922, had been the supreme Modernist poem, and everything he'd done since had represented a decline, at the end of which came *Four Quartets* which she described as a dog of a poem, a dead horse, a plastic fish.

The plastic fish description she'd borrowed from something

she'd heard another modern poet, Robert Graves, say on the BBC. Graves was asked how you knew a good poem from a bad one and he'd replied, "How do you know good fish from bad. Bad fish stinks." But then he'd gone on to say there was something worse than bad fish; there was plastic fish, that didn't smell at all. So there were good poems, bad poems, and non-poems.

Four Quartets, Sammy said, was a non-poem, an example of a true poet going through the motions after his gift – his Muse – had deserted him. It was odourless. It wasn't just dead. It had never been alive. As poet, T. S. Eliot had "lost it". Further, she claimed to have found asides in some of his essays that showed he knew he had.

Rajiv's view was exactly opposite. He saw Eliot as a poet struggling in his early work (often with the help of Buddhist and Hindu wisdom) towards "God", towards the great ascetic renunciations of *Four Quartets* which were the culmination, the achieved wisdom. In *Ash Wednesday* he'd renounced the flesh in favour of the hoped for Divine Illumination. In *Four Quartets* that Illumination had been achieved, and was represented in the image of the rose garden.

That's why Rajiv wept at the news of Eliot's marriage; why he wailed, "Bloody hell, Sammy, this man has deceived us", and asked, "Vere is his rose garden now, for goodness sake?" For a serious-minded Hindu, the renunciation of the flesh in favour of Spiritual Truth – particularly in the later years of a man's life – was something deserving of reverence; and its declaration in published poems was a solemn undertaking, not something that could be lightly cast aside. To argue as Sammy and I did (trying, really, to relieve Rajiv's distress) that you had to make a distinction between Eliot's life and his poetry made no sense to him. To renounce the flesh in poetry, and in life take your secretary to bed – it was unthinkable! It was as if Eliot had written a bad cheque. Rajiv's thesis was holed below the water line before its sails had even been unfurled.

THREE

Concerning Sammy

WHEN SAMANTHA CONLAN – SAMMY – THOUGHT BACK to the New South Wales of her childhood and youth she seemed to see it as a series of playgrounds. Peter Conlan, her father, was an orthopaedic surgeon, and when he wasn't slicing through tissue in order to saw through bone, he took an interest in the property market. He'd found for the family a big old (old for our part of the world) Federation-style bungalow in six or seven acres of bush at Beecroft, seventeen miles from central Sydney. The stud was high, the rooms airy and spacious, with polished wood floors on which his wife, Marie, put down heavy rugs – Persian in some rooms, Indian in others. The verandahs on three sides were deep and wide, and there was a huge space under the tiled roof so the house remained cool, or at least insulated against the worst of the summer heat.

Sammy and her two sisters were at home in the bush there. They learned to watch out for snakes; and more especially for funnel-web spiders, which Peter sometimes dug up in the garden, and which once or twice came into the house – squat black hairy things that reared up when challenged, ready to strike, and so deadly it was said the bite from one had killed a lion in the Taronga Park Zoo.

Peter fed the birds – kookaburras, which came down from the trees for scraps of bacon and meat he put out on fence posts; but also lorikeets and rosellas which he fed on brown sugar or bread and honey. There was always a lot of bird noise and bird colour. The currawongs strutted on the grass and made a kind of wolf-whistle. The kookaburras laughed in a way so forced and prolonged, the beginning chuckle rising to all-out hysteria, it could seem funny or frightening. The rosellas chittered in flight, all together in a crowd, very fast and seeming late for something. Sammy liked the magpies best with their undulating, burbling warble, an up-and-down sound like a river over stones.

They were in the bush in those days, but they were in Sydney. It was half a mile to shops and the railway station, and from there a comfortable train ride in to the big smoke.

Then there was the grandfather's sheep station, nearly four hundred miles away up on the Tableland, where Marie had grown up, and where they sometimes went for holidays. It was there Sammy got her first real sense of a landscape that just went on and on, tawny-brown under and blue-grey over, and where the human-seeming, despairing call of crows in the next valley frightened her because it suggested what being lost in that part of the world would mean.

Up there Sammy and her two sisters rode horses, chased wallabies, fed the chooks, learned to skin a rabbit and milk a cow, watched the shearers at work, ate huge numbers of cold chops, and talked, when nobody was looking, to "Jacky" the "Abo" rouseabout, who slept on sacks on a rough wooden frame in a shack well away from the house. "Jacky" wasn't always the same "Abo", but he was always "Jacky", and even had a permanent entry in the books that were kept for the accountant and the tax man. If there was a new "Jacky" it was because the last one had "gone walkabout", or "drunk himself silly", or "got into a bit of strife" up in town. It didn't matter who he was really; and whoever he was, though he cost next to nothing and couldn't vote because he was an "Abo", he had that entry in their grandfather's books. His home address, if that had been thought necessary, would always have been the same – the rubbish dump at the outskirts of the nearest town, where his tribe had made themselves humpies out of old sheets of wallboard and corrugated iron. And to be fair to the status of real rouseabouts, it's unlikely "Jacky" would have qualified to be called that. He was "the Abo".

The station was a place Sammy liked, but where it seemed the boy cousins were the real actors and the girls more an audience. Her favourite holiday place was Pearl Beach. Peter had bought a weekender there, and in the holidays, when he was too busy at the hospital to get away, Marie would take them – again to a house with gumtrees behind and on either side; but from the front deck, looking over pink-flowering oleanders and gold-flowering mimosa, they could see the coarse-grained yellow-orange sand of the beach, and the blue of the Pacific sending rollers in. It was wartime and there was a petrol shortage, but they had a special ration because of Peter's important work. So he would take the train in to the hospital and Marie would drive them up the coast to Pearl Beach.

Finally there was their place in the Blue Mountains. This was bought by Marie after the war when the three girls were in their teens. One of Marie's great-aunts, a maiden-lady (as unmarried women were described) died and left her a legacy. Not long afterwards Marie was visiting a friend at Katoomba and saw the house for sale. It was a sunny day, there was a beautiful garden, she had money in the bank, and she bought it.

"What on earth are we going to do with it?" Peter wanted to know.

"I'll think of something," Marie said.

She found a local woman, a widow, who agreed to live there, keep the house clean and tidy, tend the garden and, when the family visited, cook for them. For all of that she received what was called "a small retainer". Her principal payment was that she could live there rent free.

The house, which had its name, *Vallamont*, inscribed in curly letters on marble over its front verandah, was somewhere Marie could go when she wanted to be free of Peter, whose presence, if prolonged, and especially when he was in buoyant good humour, made her irritable.

"In the mountains, *there* you feel free," he would say to her in a mocking voice. It was some years before Sammy discovered that it was a line from *The Waste Land*, and that it was especially apt, because of the lines that come before:

> He said Marie,
> Marie, hold on tight. And down we went.
> In the mountains, there you feel free.

Marie loved that house – or she loved at least the *idea* of it – because Katoomba, like the part of the Tableland where she grew up, was more than three thousand feet above sea level. She liked cold winter nights and clear sunny days. But she could never quite take on board that although there were similarities, there were differences too. It was much wetter in

34

the mountains. When the rains came she grumbled, and Peter teased her, saying the Almighty had let her down again.

"My mother's an awful grumbler," Sammy told me. "And Peter – he's temperamentally a mocker. They're a bad combination – always have been."

Marie's house was at the end of a road at the edge of the town. Where the road ended, a track went down through trees, crossed a creek and a park, and brought you to a series of walking paths that led to what the three girls used to call the Big Drop. The plateau simply came to a stop. There was a fall that Sammy thought might have been fifteen hundred or two thousand feet; and directly below the landscape, more or less horizontal, dense in bush, impenetrable, continued on its way.

Sometimes Sammy and her sisters would go to the clifftop in the early morning and discover that the lower landscape had vanished under white cloud that lay over it like scoured fleeces, with only a couple of summits poking through, while they looked down from above in crystal-clear air and bright sunlight. Later Sammy was to read in a novel by Saul Bellow the reflection that we of the air-flight age were the first to have looked *down* on clouds. It was a thought Joni Mitchell was to turn into a song.

"But I'd done it," Sammy protested, "before I ever went in a plane. And so had the Aborigines of that region, for thousands of years."

And then as day advanced the cloud would evaporate, and there it was, the landscape stretching away into the distance, a huge chunk (but really only a tiny fragment) of Terra Australis Incognito.

No matter how often Sammy went there, it was always a

shock. She would tell herself she knew how huge the drop was and how vast the landscape, and that this time she wouldn't (she would *not*) be surprised; and each time the surprise was the same. In places streams came to an edge and simply fell over in cascades. Far below, the tops of the blue gum forest were dotted with white spots which were really cockatoos, big white birds with bright yellow crests and yellow underwings, whose territorial screaming is one of the harshest sounds in nature, rivalled only, perhaps, by the braying of a donkey.

The cockatoos were up on the heights as well, and fiercely territorial. Sammy used to describe – and act out – one of these big birds trying to dislodge a kookaburra from a dead tree: fanning its wing feathers, lifting its crest, screeching, swooping and darting at its rival, while the kookaburra sat quite still and unruffled, only turning its huge black beak as if to say, "If you really want to run on my sword, mate . . ."

By the time her mother had bought the house in the Blue Mountains Sammy was already enrolled as a boarder at Fresley Ladies College where, although it was an expensive institution intended for girls from affluent families, the dormitories were the building's open verandahs. This exposure to fresh air, like cold showers at British-style boarding schools for boys, was considered "healthy" – bracing both physically and morally. In severe weather, when the wind and rain drove in, canvas rollers came down to keep the beds dry. But there was no protection (apart from blankets and hot water bottles) from the chill of winter nights; and nothing but getting under the sheet to keep yourself from mosquitoes in summer.

Sammy didn't talk much about Fresley. Considering she'd spent five years there, she said, it was more of a blank in her life than it ought to have been. But once she told me her worst memory of the school, and her best.

Worst was being rostered "on Tins" as a punishment for "being smart". The geography teacher had said they were to have a lesson on Nicaragua, and Sammy, remembering a popular song, immediately launched into the opening lines –

"Managua Nicaragua is a wonderful spot,
There's coffee and bananas and the temperature's hot."

This brought laughter from the class and rage from the teacher. Sammy was hauled out and berated. She was puzzled at first, then indignant – and the indignation remained, because really, far from "being smart", she'd thought she was offering something. It had struck her as amusing that the popular song was itself like a mini-lesson in geography; and afterwards she even wondered whether that was the problem – that it had put into an entertaining nutshell most of what the teacher had to say on the subject.

The punishment was that she had to be "on Tins" for a week. This meant that each day she had to empty used sanitary napkins from tins in the lavatories, wrap them all together in newspaper, and take them to the incinerator and burn them. The smell of the blood-soaked napkins made her feel ill. The burning, fusing the original stale blood smell with acrid smoke, was worse. It became Sammy's notion of what the smoke from Auschwitz's crematorium chimneys might have been like.

Her best experience at Fresley was the discovery of T. S. Eliot and *The Waste Land*. By the time this happened she was already a great reader – of poetry as well as fiction. There had been for her the discovery of traditional favourites like "The Lady of Shallot", "Kubla Khan", "Tintern Abbey", "La Belle Dame Sans Merci"; and then came "the defining moment" (as she liked to call it) when an English teacher, supervising them in the library rather than in the classroom, had said, "Girls, listen please."

Sammy remembered looking up and seeing the sun coming down through high windows on to the shining heads while the teacher read, in a beautiful, rather deep and resonant voice, the passage from *The Waste Land* that begins:

> The river's tent is broken: the last fingers of leaf
> Clutch and sink into the wet bank. The wind
> Crosses the brown land unheard.

The river's *tent* is broken! There was a lurch in the stomach and a prickling of the scalp, a feeling unfamiliar and almost too physical, almost unwelcome.

Something was happening to her. She was entering a new world, and the key attached to it was the name T. S. Eliot.

So she read the poem – many times; and one of its minor and incidental rewards was to pick up the point of her father's joke about Marie and the mountains.

> He said Marie,
> Marie, hold on tight, and down we went.
> In the mountains, there you feel free.

– which was followed by the strangely resonant, perhaps sinister, line:

> I read, much of the night, and go south in the winter.

*

For Sammy the Blue Mountains were a mythical landscape, mysterious, like poetry itself. And then to add to that excitement came the discovery that near the house Marie had bought lived a writer – Eleanor Dark.

Sammy had read Australian books and poems; but by this time she was writing poems and stories of her own, and to discover a real writer, one who could be seen pottering in her garden and saying goodbye to her husband, Dr Dark, as he drove off to do his rounds, was something new. It made writing something real, done by real people, right there in Australia.

In Katoomba, she soon discovered, there was endless talk about the Darks –dark talk. They were said to be communists, even possibly spies. The little town buzzed, many deploring their presence, some tolerant, a few admiring, all pleased because the author of books like *The Timeless Land* (everyone seemed to have heard of that one – none, or none Sammy met, to have read it) brought a certain aura of fame to the locality, and something to talk about other than the weather. Politically Sammy's own family were right wing, Peter a supporter of the Liberal half of the Coalition, Marie one of the good old Country Party faithful. There was no grief at their house when Mr Chifley, the Labour Prime Minister, died, and there was cheering when Mr Menzies – "Pig-Iron Bob" – defeated Dr Evatt.

Throughout Sammy's teen years she had been in a state of inner revolt – against the family, against Fresley, against her own pampered life. But until she learned of Eleanor Dark, the writer, and her husband Dr Dark, it hadn't occurred to her that that might be the way to go. Politics! She became at once a supporter of Labour – even, maybe, "in theory" (though she didn't at that time know what the theory of it was) of communism. Now her rebellion had focus. Back at Fresley she gathered around her a group of like-minded rebels who would give their teachers and their parents something new to worry about.

If this rebellion had an emotional target it was (of course) her parents, Marie especially. Sammy would have said in those years that she hated her mother. She believed that she did; and on reflection in London, seven or eight years later, she had to concede that the difference between believing you hate your mother and actually hating her is fine. Possibly Marie hated Sammy – but Sammy didn't think so. It was "natural", she said, for a daughter to hate her mother; "unnatural" for the hate to be returned.

Sammy did worry about her own hostility, especially when her sisters (whom, however, she believed their mother favoured) told her she was cruel and was making Marie unhappy. She accepted that it was something she should work on, fight against; and during the middle term of her last year at Fresley she set out to force a change in herself; to appreciate her mother by imagining she'd died. Over and over Sammy told herself that Marie was dead – killed in a road accident/a plane crash/of cancer/cardiac arrest/snake bite/spider bite/food poisoning/raped-and-murdered/pushed off the cliffs at Katoomba . . . by Peter? At which she would laugh.

So at first it didn't work. Either she didn't believe in the death; or just for a moment she did, and thought it no bad thing. The bizarre and terrible ends she invented for her mother amused her; and once, suddenly laughing in the classroom, and asked by the English mistress to explain what was so funny, her laughing fit was increased by the recognition that the teacher's name was Miss Body. Still pressed to explain, the eyes of the whole class on her, she said in a reckless and provocative outburst of truthfulness, that she'd just imagined her mother had fallen off the Manley ferry wearing yellow gumboots.

She escaped "Tins" on that occasion only because it was a punishment from which senior girls were exempt; but she was set to copy out "Five Bells", Kenneth Slessor's elegy for a friend drowned in Sydney Harbour.

But Sammy didn't give up. She focused now, solemnly, with fierce concentration, on just one kind of death – a car accident (very likely given Marie's erratic driving), and gradually it began to enter her imagination, and even her dreams, as something that had really happened. Grief crept up on her, taking a hold which, though incomplete, was sufficient to mean she had sometimes to go away and weep behind a bookstack in the library, or in a quiet corner of the garden, or in her wind-swept bed on the verandah.

So she went home at the end of term feeling what a good girl should – that she loved her mother. She was all over Marie, hugging and kissing her, which Marie didn't like; making her cups of tea and offering to do chores. "What have you been up to?" Marie wanted to know. "What've you got on your conscience?" And then, "You're not pregnant are you, Sammy?"

There was a blazing row, after which, exhausted and weighed down with guilt, Sammy found herself once again hating her mother.

Fresley had given her a taste for poetry and fiction, but she'd learned very little about modern Australian writing; so when she enrolled at Sydney University as a B.A. student, she decided she had some catching up to do. She did it mostly on her own, in libraries ("the Fisher" and "the Mitchell" became important locations on the map of her life), and in bookshops. She discovered literary periodicals with names like *Meanjin* and *Jindyworobak*. There was also the Sydney Bulletin's Red Page, with a literary life of its own separate from the rest of the paper that still carried its old banner, "Australia for the White Man". She sent the Bulletin some of her poems, typed on her new portable Olivetti (Peter's present to celebrate her enrolling as a student). They came back, usually with printed rejection slips, once or twice with kind, faintly encouraging notes from the editor Douglas Stewart.

Her first published pieces were articles, and one or two poems, written for the student newspaper, *honi soit*, which issued from an outhouse on the lawn of the student union; and it was through *honi soit* that she met Friedrich Goldstein, a young *Sydney Morning Herald* journalist invited along to talk to those who were putting the paper together and were interested in a career in journalism.

"Friedrich distinctly German, and Goldstein distinctly Jewish," someone in the *honi soit* office remarked; but was that right? The man who came to speak to them was blond and blue eyed, with a look, Sammy thought, of the Australian tennis champion of those years, John Bromwich – the man with the famous double-handed backhand.

Freddy had a pleasant voice, a slight New Zealand accent but with an edge of European foreignness. He talked about type-faces, and setting up a page. To Sammy he appeared somewhat nervous, but civilized, articulate, intelligent, attractive; and (there was no doubt about it – he didn't try to conceal it) she was the person in the room he noticed, found interesting, wanted to impress.

Sammy said nothing, contributed nothing at all except her full attention. When the talk and the questions were over she moved, not too close, but where he could speak to her if he wanted. He did want. They had coffee together. Then, because of something she'd said about an out-of-print book she hadn't been able to find, he took her to a second-hand bookshop in Glebe.

They walked along the streets, talking, losing their way and in no hurry to find it again. He told her about his family, confirmed that it was Jewish on the father's side. His mother was Aryan German; and it was from her he'd inherited his blond hair and blue eyes. They had gone from Germany to Palestine to escape the Nazis, and then from Palestine to New Zealand. He and his father were among the few survivors of a family of uncles and aunts and cousins and grandparents, most of whom had gone to the gas chambers.

He said that although English was his only language, *there was also for him German*, which he'd spoken as an infant; and although he'd lost it, because his father would not allow it to be spoken, it wasn't gone absolutely. He thought of it as a shadowy "other" vocabulary and grammar, like a hovering ghost, almost invisible. What this meant, he said, was that he spoke his second language. His first had been lost.

They'd been walking for some time, and as he told her this, stopping a moment in the street and looking at her intently, she could see over his shoulder, and over the shoulders of houses, the iron bow of the Coat Hanger. And the way he said "But there is also for me German" seemed to her to illustrate the point – unconsciously, because he would not, she

43

thought, have recognized the foreignness that was somehow there in that arrangement of words. "But zere is alzo for me German," she repeated in her head, adding for emphasis a comic accent which Freddy didn't have.

He made a strong impression, this man with a whole language locked up inside him, because he was a part of History – of what she had begun to think of as "the bigger picture". And the bigger picture for her had to include the Holocaust. That, she would acknowledge later, had always been one element – but only one – in what had drawn her to Freddy Goldstein. This was a man who as a child, if his parents had remained in Germany, would have suffered the humiliation of the yellow star, the nightmare of the cattle wagons, and the final horror of the gas chamber.

This thought perhaps showed a moment on Sammy's face, making Freddy think he'd been too serious about his lost language, because now he said he would tell her a story about the German language.

"It's quite unfair to the language," he said, "but it's funny. Well . . ." He hesitated, looking at her still serious face. Did she have a sense of humour? "I think it's funny."

A Frenchman, an Italian, an Englishman and a German (so the story went), were arguing in a park or garden about which of them had the most beautiful language. The Frenchman was convinced that his was superior; and, noticing a butterfly among the flowers, he gave as an example the word *papillon*. "*Papillon*," he said, flapping imaginary wings, dancing and floating from flower to flower. "*Papillon. Papillon.*"

Yes beautiful, the Italian agreed. Very fine. But think of the same word in Italian. It was even prettier: "*Farfallo. Farfallo.*" And he too flapped and glided around, acting it out.

The Englishman didn't feel his language had been put into the shade by these examples. Butterfly. Wasn't that quite as delicate and expressive? And he joined the other two, the *papillon* and the *farfallo*, saying "Butterfly. Butterfly."

But what about the German?

As he told the story Freddy Goldstein had been acting it out, flapping and gliding among imaginary flowers. Now he stood, stiffly to attention, staring ahead with slightly mad eyes.

"Then all three notice" (he went on) "that the German is standing like this – saying nothing. They stop being butterflies and look at him. There's a long silence until, all at once, the German barks in a parade-ground voice, 'And vot is wrong vith *schmetterling*?'"

FOUR

And then there was Margot

THE DATE OF MY WRITER'S BLOCK, RIGHT AT THE beginning of the new century, was significant. There was a century of history I carried within myself which in some sense *was* myself. Half of it, as I've said, I'd lived through with an adult consciousness. Half I'd learned from the horse's mouth – parents, grandparents, older friends, old soldiers; and from reading. From people had come stories, memories and impressions – direct, fragmentary, heat from the furnace. From reading had come the bigger picture, context, "cause". (Twentieth-Century History Question One: What were the causes of the First World War?)

This narrative, myth, or fairy-tale, this history of the century just finished, had been the story I knew best, went on learning, and had to tell myself over and over in my writing, each time with a different emphasis. It was in a way my dreamlife, because it's only by dreaming (though the dream is founded on the facts) that reality is grasped. "Tread softly, for you tread on my dreams."

And strangely, it was the second half of the story, the half I'd been part of, that could sometimes seem less significant, less interesting, less momentous – a long aftermath rather than a dénouement. It was as if the twentieth century had ended with the bullet in Hitler's brain, the opening of the Nazi death camps, and the dropping of two atomic bombs. Since then we'd all been in school, trying to learn the lessons, squabbling about what it all meant and where to go next, not quite daring (thankfully) to let our biggest mistakes repeat themselves.

But if this was the story beneath all my stories, there was another fact, equally important which I now, in my "blocked" state, reflected on. It was what in the movie- making and screenplay writing business is called POV – point of view. Always in my writing the perspective had been determined by what was for me home base, Auckland, New Zealand, a place which, seen from almost anywhere else, was the perimeter, the periphery, an outpost, a backwater – away *over there*, and away *down under*. Even when I wrote stories set in other places, Britain or North America, Italy or France, still it was as my feet were planted somewhere on Tamaki-Makau-Rau, "the Place of a Thousand Lovers", this rain-swept sun-stroked volcanic isthmus between two harbours, the Waitemata and the Manukau.

In my early years at school, when the Second World War was being fought, a very large map of the world hung at the front of the classroom (so *educative* – unimaginable now!), a Mercator's projection showing the British Empire in red – "the Empire," (the teacher told us, tracing the sun's path with her wooden pointer) "on which the sun never sets."

You could say that that Empire, for all its flailings and failings, the damage it inflicted, its misrepresentation of itself to itself and to those it imposed upon, none the less made us part of a larger world, something our new independence (though of course we must have it) can never do. To have on your passport, as we did in my youth, "British

Subject, New Zealand Citizen" may have seemed demeaning. National pride was sure to rebel, and in due course did. But that was truly a *passport*, as one's "Uruwhenua" of the present day, with its "Nationality: New Zealand", and its texts in English and Maori, is not. Uruwhenua! The Empire had its absurdities, its sacred nonsense which it was impiety to question or challenge – and we have replaced them with our own. That is Human Progress. We move forward always; and our capacity for folly, ever-changing, ever-fresh, moves with us and takes new forms.

But what I remember noticing especially about that map was that New Zealand was represented twice, once at the lower right corner, and again at the lower left. It was something the teacher never mentioned, perhaps because it would have been too difficult to explain; perhaps, even, because she couldn't explain it. When referring to our own country she pointed always to the lower right-hand New Zealand – the one which, seen on this scale, appeared to be just offshore from Australia – as if other wasn't there.

Another child might have thought that to have your country shown twice on the map of the world when everyone else was there just once signified our importance. I felt, rather, the reverse, but in a way that wasn't without a certain thrill. You couldn't have a map with Europe on it twice, or America, or Africa. But we were so insignificant, so small, so "off the map" and "out of the picture", it didn't matter! We were doubly, *uniquely*, unimportant.

"Remoteness" in those days, and on into my young adult years, was a preoccupation – of New Zealand intellectuals especially. Travel (once the war was over) was for the rich, the privileged, and the lucky. From Auckland to London took four and a half or five weeks by sea. "Distance looks our way," a New Zealand poet wrote in a silly and often quoted line. It didn't. We looked its way, and it seldom looked back.

It was not just that we were in the Southern Hemisphere, where the sun went around to the north, the moon was "upside down", and Christmas came with the longest days of summer. It was *where* we were in the South that made our position extreme. From that lower right corner of Mercator's map we looked north and west to what Europe called "the East"; from the lower left we looked north and east to what Europe called "the West".

So – to put it more starkly than is quite fair, but for the sake of the simplicity and boldness with which these late reflections on my own career came to me – my years of full consciousness had been the years of what I'd come to think of as the twentieth century's "aftermath"; and my perch of observation had been one of maximum insignificance, second only to the moon. Born into a "client culture", heir to colonialism's stolen goods, innocent inheritor of a history of guilt, I was committed to an art whose future seemed uncertain, and with stories to tell which I had never had any good reason to suppose anyone would want to listen to.

As these reflections came to me it seemed logical that they should confirm my writer's block. Time to give up, take a rest, put myself out to grass. Time for the gym, the kitset house, the bicycle tour; time for wine in France, and Death in Venice.B

But the effect, like that childhood recognition of New Zealand's supreme unimportance, was quite different. I felt liberated. I had no prospects, had never had any, and therefore had no one to answer to but myself, or to God (who didn't exist). By the time of Otto Stiltz's phone call, and of our visit to his stratospheric apartment, I was ready – and when one is ready, one sees what otherwise passes unnoticed.

Here, out of the blue, was "Rumpelstiltskin with Hitler's nose", the "ex" of Samantha Conlan – of Sammy who had been the great love of his life, and perhaps the lost love of mine. A door had opened on a piece of my past I thought I'd lost.

But I must not jump ahead of my story. If in time I was to come to think of Sammy as a "lost love", that was a realization which would arrive only slowly. At first, and for a long time, I was to see her as she saw herself, a young woman in love and in pain, desperately involved with a married man, pretending to run away from him so she would not seem to be running after him, but running only slowly and along a path she knew he was soon to take.

Friedrich Goldstein was Sam's lover. I, on the other hand, was her patient playmate, her kind listener, the one she trusted. I was also unpractised in love, accepted my role, and only recognized later, looking back, how the agitation that went with it – the arousal and denial – made me confused, discontented, and soon put into my head that I too had to have a lover. Am I blaming Sam (but there is no blame) for my affair with the formidable Margot Derry?

Margot, another New Zealander, was one of those young women at Castlenau Mansions. I noticed her at once for one reason especially, because she was intelligent. We were all intelligent, I suppose, but Margot was exceptional. Not assertive, just impressively knowledgable, and precise in a way that seemed somewhat patrician, every word clear and bell–like, every sentence having a beginning, a middle and an end, so when you said something careless and she questioned it, or corrected you, it gave you the feeling, not so much of having been stupid as of having said something socially unacceptable – a breach of decorum, a failure of tone. She was inclined to be prim, at least in manner. But she was also amusing, witty, with a ready musical laugh.

It's often said that men shy clear of intelligent women, but it seems to me, after many years of close observation, that intelligence exerts a powerful sexual attraction both ways. Human beings are programmed to breed with the best available; and even the less clever recognize and are attracted to intelligence, just as the plain are attracted to beauty. I was, I knew quite well, less intelligent than Margot, and a great deal less beautiful, so I didn't rate my chances as good; but I was drawn to her – not as the moth to the flame; more, perhaps, in the spirit of the mountain climber to the highest peak.

There was one other thing which gave us a kind of rapport and something to talk about. From the first moment of seeing one another she and I both felt that we'd met before, but neither could remember where or when, and in the end it became one of those jokes shared around among the group. Margot and Laszlo, it was understood, had known one another in a past life.

But my friendship with her, and my attempts to ingratiate myself, got off to a bad start. Like me, Margot was only temporarily at the Hammersmith flat. Soon she was to take up a scholarship at Oxford, and already she was going there and returning, making arrangements for admission to St Anne's. Alone in the flat one day during her absence, I noticed a letter on her bed. It was from New Zealand and I read it.

No qualms? To tell the truth no, there were none. The letter was there, no one was about, and I read it. End of story.

A couple of days later four or five of us were sitting talking around the big kitchen table. At first the conversation was about kinds of spoken English, and included imitations of one another's accents. It was remarked, for example, that I referred to my own country as Niew Zillon, and particularly liked igg sendwiches; and that Petra Neutz, who came from Sethufrica, was worried about Bleck prytest. I recounted how a taxi driver in Sydney, when I told him I was on my way to London, had said I might see the Coin on her horse riding down the Mall. And Sammy and I exchanged traditional cross-Tasman jokes about her Seedney Breedge and my Sudney Brudge. Then we turned to English English, and everyone tried to do the BBC accent which at that time was unvarying and posh. Margot's was the most accurate, Rajiv's the funniest: "Hyah is the nyaws read by Jodrell Bank. In the Hiyse of Cummins the softernoon . . ."

So we were all very relaxed. And then, as the conversation wandered away from language, something someone said prompted me to recount an exceptional event. I told them I'd heard or read – quite recently, but couldn't remember where – about someone in New Zealand who had been . . . or whose house/car/cat/farm/mother-in-law had been . . .

The point is that I can't any longer remember what the exceptional event was. What I do remember is my intense embarrassment and sense of exposure when I'd finished my account and Margot, looking at me across the table, frowning, still deciding what she should make of this, said, "That's odd. Someone just told me that same story." She paused a moment, and then added, "In a letter."

It wouldn't have been so bad if I'd kept my head. I might have murmured, "Coincidence. Mmm, yes. Remarkable." Or said nothing. Or perhaps invented (it would have been difficult) my own separate source for the story. Instead I blurted out, "Oh my godfather," slapped my forehead, stood up as if to rush from the room, and then sat down again.

Next morning, while Rajiv and I were still dozing in our sleeping bags on cushions on the sitting room floor, I heard the mail arriving – the Pushing Through, the Slot-Flap Rattle, the Floor-Board Thud – one of those inconsequential and curiously exciting sequences of sound (another was the Start-Up and Whirr-Away of the milkman's electric cart under the window) that signalled one was waking, not at home in New Zealand, where mail and milk were delivered to a box at a gate some way from the house, but in "the Old Country".

I rolled over in time to see Margot go past our half-open door, pulling back from her face the wavy brown hair that would soon be parted in the middle and pinned and clasped into an orderly state. There was a quiet shuffling while she went through the mail, then back she came with several items in one hand and a single letter in the other. She pushed our door wider and leaned on the jamb, the hair tumbling forward again around her clever face. "Nothing for you two," she said. "But there's this one, Laszlo." She waved it. "It's for me. D'you mind very much if I read it first?"

I had nothing to lose. Taking a step forward rather than back, I said, "It was a short-cut, Margot. I wanted to get to know you."

For an instant response this was, I think, pretty good, and an illustration of how fast and efficient the mind can be when it works in close conjunction with the heart and the hormones.

At a stroke I'd avoided the pretence of incomprehension, the dishonesty of denial, and the charade of remorse; I'd skipped over the confession, implied the apology, and gone straight to the explanation – one which flattered her *and was truthful!*

She seemed to appreciate all this. Her keen eyes flickered a moment directly on to me, and her expression, although not yet ready to relinquish disapproval, was amused. She stood a moment at the door, half-smiling; then moved on down the corridor. Over her shoulder she said, "Please stay out of my bedroom." It didn't sound terribly forbidding.

FIVE

An Encounter in Russell Square

I REMEMBER WHEN I WAS FIRST IN LONDON MY
astonishment at the size of the stone lions at the back of
the British Museum, and the silliness of the expressions on
their faces. The bronze ones in Trafalgar Square were even
larger. Why such emphasis on a beast that never inhabited
"England's green and pleasant land"? And why those absurd
expressions of disdain, which did indeed look English?

Rajiv, on the other hand, thought it appropriate that they
should be lions, that they should be larger-than-life, and that
they should have a look (as he saw it) of regal superiority. In
fact, he insisted, their size was no more than adequate. They
were symbols of imperial power, and imperial power could
not be expected to represent itself merely life size, nor in the
image of the fox, the snake, the stoat, the pussy cat.

Equally I recall his deep disappointment when we went
together to see Buckingham Palace for the first time. To
both of us it was a familiar image from newspapers and books
of our childhood; and especially from newsreels of VE Day –
the day following the German unconditional surrender – with
Winston Churchill joining the King and Queen and the two
Princesses (they were known as Elizabeth and Margaret Rose,
but might at that moment have been re-named Happy and

Glorious) to wave from the balcony to cheering multitudes. Rajiv's memories exactly coincided with my own; but to him the real Palace was so much smaller than the Palace of his imagination, he thought at first we must have come to the wrong address.

"Goodness gracious Laszlo," he said, "this is a palace for a minor Maharaja."

Rajiv was used to grandeur. I, whose childhood notion of architectural splendour had been the Auckland Railway Station, was not. "It looks pretty damn' big to me," I said.

He went on shaking his head, murmuring, "No, no, no, no." This was not remotely adequate for Her Britannic Majesty.

It was not that Rajiv approved of the British Empire — quite the reverse. He saw the return of self-rule to the Indian sub-continent as the restoration of stolen goods; and there was still a resentment, an injured pride, half buried, but distinctly there in his personality, at the knowledge that *his* people had been for so long ruled by what he thought of (I didn't quite) as *my* people. But this fact, this history of India's subjugation, would have been much harder to accept if the Imperial rulers had not at least behaved like masters, with pomp and ceremony, authority and grandeur. So Rajiv liked his lions big and disdainful, and would have wished the Palace on a proper scale to represent the power India had yielded to.

It was something I didn't fully grasp until we were walking away, back along the Mall under the splendid late-summer trees. "It can't have been real power," I said. "How could a few men in big shorts and solar topees have ruled tens of millions? It must have been bluff."

"Please," Rajiv said, "do not insult us. And kindly do not speak to me of this subject any more."

We had arrived in London, Rajiv and Sammy and I, at a time when the British Empire was cracking, crumbling, falling apart, to be reassembled into something nebulous and inglorious that was already being called the Commonwealth. There was the Mau Mau rebellion in Kenya, unrest and riot in Northern and Southern Rhodesia and in Nyasaland, rumblings and stirrings in British Guyana, trouble in Cyprus where British military service conscripts were being taunted and stoned. And that first year, 1956, was the year of "Suez".

Here is what happened: Colonel Gamal Abdel Nasser (how promptly that search for a name was answered, while calls on the short-term memory go unanswered!) of Egypt "nationalized" the Suez Canal — claimed it, in other words, as Egypt's own — and Britain, in one of those outrage-reflexes of the dying lion, decided he had to be stopped. So the British Government got together in secret with the French and with the government of the new state of Israel, to concoct a reason for military intervention. Israel would attack Egypt, and Britain and France would mobilize their military forces to "separate the belligerents". That this had been cooked up in advance was indignantly denied, and the denials would go on for years, for decades, until the events were so far in the past, and the major actors in the melodrama so uniformly dead, there was no point in denying any longer.

Sammy and I joined the protests. She was uneasy because of Israel's involvement. Freddy Goldstein was always in her mind, and she knew that what had happened to the Jews in Europe required one to be especially understanding of what

Israel judged it had to do to protect itself. But the blatant lies upset her; and worse than the lies, the idiocy of the newspapers and the people who believed them. We stood outside 10 Downing Street with placards. (In those days you could do that – there were no gates barring the way.) We joined a huge rally in Trafalgar Square, and surged with it down into Whitehall. Charged by mounted police, the duffle coats stood their ground, calling "Shame! Shame!" in a deep lugubrious collective voice. It was the *other* British voice – the voice of weary Honour and Self-Reproach.

Of course protest would have achieved nothing if the military ruse had worked, but it didn't – came to nothing because of a very simple mistake. The action had not been cleared first with the Americans, who never minded *realpolitik* so long as it was their own, or had their approval in advance. President Eisenhower refused to support this adventure of Prime Minister Eden's. America opposed it in the UN, and the troops had to be called home.

So the Suez Canal was now Colonel Nasser's. It had been said by Eden and his Tory cohort, and echoed by the Tory papers, that Egypt would be incapable of running the Canal – that it would fall into ruin, that one of the world's great trade routes would be lost, that it was Britain's "heavy responsibility" to preserve it, that the alternative was (dread word from the days of Hitler) "appeasement" of the dictator Nasser. Perhaps the Club-chaps and pub-lads who echoed these things even believed them. It didn't occur to them that the Egyptians were the same race that had built the pyramids. The military detritus was cleared away, the sunken shipping removed, and the Canal operated once again, as safely and efficiently as before, but the returns now went to the nation through whose territory it had been cut.

Soon (perhaps in the following year) Eden himself was also cleared away – out of Downing Street and off to that old-toy cupboard, the House of Lords. Rab Butler, the Tory we thought of (I no longer remember why) as the deserving one, was shunted off to one side, and Harold Macmillan became Prime Minister – "Supermac", the man who would speak famously of "the winds of change" in Africa, and win elections at home with the shamelessly racy slogan, "You've never had it so good".

But politics was a small part of our lives. Sammy, Rajiv and I used to meet over coffee or for lunch. We went together to plays, public lectures, recitals. Sometimes Rajiv cooked us a meal in his digs. He kept some of the ingredients in the bottom drawer of the dressing table in his bedroom, which was just through the door from his little linoleum-floored kitchen. They were spices, herbs, seeds, nuts, each in a square of white Indian cotton, knotted at the top, and brought among his cabin luggage from Bombay. He kept the dishes mild for us; and when we told him how much we enjoyed them he said, "Good good good so you can taste it then? You British have such refined palates." It was a remark which set him chuckling, while Sammy and I protested that we were not British.

We ate the meal sitting on the back steps which ran down from his kitchen into a wall-enclosed garden, with fruit trees, scruffy grass, an overgrown vegetable patch, and a small glass-house with broken frames. Over it all spread the limbs of huge trees in neighbouring gardens. There was that stillness of long evenings in a London summer, something that was new to me, coming as I did from an isthmus where even the mildest summer air is always restless, the leaves never still, and where the twilight doesn't last. And it was probably my earliest discovery of that *other* London, that secret territory, home of birds, squirrels and foxes, children, flowers and vegetable patches, which often lies hidden from the streets behind the grim brick façades of terrace-houses.

Rajiv worked mostly at the British Museum Reading Room; I was more often at the Senate House Library. Sammy loved the Reading Room. But she liked also to range about, to find places where famous modern writers had lived, pubs they frequented, bookshops where they'd met and read their poems. These places, I assumed, were going into her *Secret History of Modernism*.

After the disillusion caused by T. S. Eliot's marriage to Valerie Fletcher, Rajiv talked to his supervisor, a brisk and practical Senior Lecturer at UCL, and the subject of his research was changed. The Irish poet W. B. Yeats, they decided, suited him better than Eliot. Yeats had been influenced by Eastern thought, which he was able to understand (so Rajiv now argued) because, unlike Eliot, he was free of any Christian influence. He had conducted researches into communication with the spirit world. He had taken astrology very seriously, even constructing a whole system of human history based on the movements of the moon, stars and planets.

"Yeats was no ascetic," Sammy warned. She'd heard somewhere that in his old age the Irish poet had been a famous philanderer, and she didn't want Rajiv suffering another disappointment.

"Oh yes but that is OK," Rajiv said in his rolling up-and-down speech which ran a sentence together so it sounded like a single very long word. "He liked young vimmin I know that. But he did not deceive himself. His way to God was the way of the world. The world was his emblem for what was beyond."

As for Sammy – her obsession with Eliot's poetry was not diminishing. She was tormented by the thought that any day of the week he might be sitting in an office only a quarter of a mile from where she was studying every word she could find of his earliest publications. She longed at the very least to see him. Every morning she came by tube on the Piccadilly Line from Hammersmith, arriving at Russell Square and walking very slowly past the offices of Faber and Faber (they were then at number 24) in the hope that she might encounter him.

But her view of him was complicated by the immovable conviction that his Muse had deserted him; and more, by his anti-Semitism. This was widely known, but it was spoken about seldom and circumspectly. By now – post-Second World War, post-Holocaust – Eliot must have come to regret, for example, the series of lectures in which he'd argued that "any large number of free thinking Jews" in a society was "undesirable". Published in 1934, after Hitler had come to power, these could only have been meant to signal approval of the anti-Jewish measures then coming into force in Germany.

Those lectures were not allowed to be reprinted. And the 'jew' in the poem "Gerontion" was re-spelled "Jew". But nothing could be done about the fact that, with or without the upper case J, the Jew in that poem was described as having been "spawned in some estaminet of Antwerp". Nothing could be done about the figure of "Bleistein" in another of the poems, the "Chicago Semite Viennese" whose "lustreless protrusive eye / Stares from the protozoic slime"; nor (apart from again correcting the j to upper case) about the lines

> The rats are underneath the piles.
> The jew is underneath the lot;

nor about "Rachel *née* Rabinovitch" who, in yet another poem, "tears at the grapes with murderous claws". These caricature Jews, who would hardly have been out of place in a Nazi propaganda movie of the 1930s, were there in his *Collected Poems*. They were in the public domain, immoveable evidence of a phobia (and not a mild one) – the same phobia that had sent the six million to cruel execution.

Nothing for poor Tom Eliot to do but sit it out in a posture of "everyone makes mistakes". And most of his critics and fellow-writers were being "decent" about it. He wasn't held to account. They looked the other way, coughed nervously, spoke of other things. Sam too tried to forgive, or anyway to forget, that aspect of his work.

"How unpleasant to meet Mr Eliot", he had written in one of his comic poems. Each morning, walking slowly past 24 Russell Square, she hoped for the good luck to have that "unpleasantness" visited upon her – to see the handsome and famous Mr Eliot, his hook-nose and homburg, his anxious frown, his fastidious mouth, his large wide-spaced darkly intelligent eyes. She wasn't sure what she would do if he appeared. Stare? Ask for an autograph? Try to tell him what *The Waste Land* meant to her? Tell him she knew his secret – that he'd "lost it" – but that it was safe with her?

One day (I think it was just before the marriage announcement which caused Rajiv to change tack with his research),

Sammy was going through issues of the *Criterion*, the literary journal Eliot had edited in the 1930s, when she came on a review of a book that had tried to alert the world to what was happening to the German Jews. The review was unsigned; but it mocked the book, accusing its authors of "sensationalism". Worse, because of the style Sammy believed Eliot himself had written it. This seemed to her worse than all the other examples of his anti-Semitism; because here was a cry for help being carried to the world from Hitler's Germany before the Final Solution was really under way, before the death camps had been established, but at a time when the writing was clearly on the wall; and this cry had been derided in a journal Eliot was responsible for, perhaps even in words he himself had written.

Sam's indignation that day was huge. Sheltering with me under the portico at the front of the Museum where I went to smoke my Woodbines, she could scarcely keep still. She talked, marched away from me as if compelled into motion, then back again because she had more to say.

Now, she assured me, she had a new resolution. If, sooner or later, she did meet T. S. Eliot, ("And sooner or later I will," she added fiercely) she would ask whether he was the author of this review. She would also suggest that whether he or another wrote it, he should be ashamed of having published it. She had copied it out and typed it up, and she would carry the copy with her always, so that if he argued with her about what it said or implied, she would be able to quote from it directly. "He won't wriggle out of it," she said. "He's a dog and I'm going to tell him he is."

In the next while Sammy ran through this encounter often in her head; carried her copy of the review, read it over and thought out exactly what she would say so it could be got through quickly before he'd escaped.

But the more carefully she prepared for it, the more improbable and unreal this meeting seemed. It was becoming like one of those dreams in which you find yourself with the Queen, or your favourite Hollywood Star, and have a pleasant chat; or with some wrong-doing politician, and put him in his place. She went on looking for Eliot in the mornings, but she stopped believing she would see him.

This must have been Autumn or early winter, and at that time of year (this was before London's Clean Air Act had begun to work its magic) there used to be from time to time a "pea-souper" – the kind of fog so heavy and thick old people and sickly children died, birds fell out of the sky, and if you had a long arm you could stretch it out in front of you and watch your hand vanish from sight. It was a dampened down world of looming yellow fog-lights, of wailing river-boat sirens, of air which wasn't air and which, although not altogether unpleasant, sometimes wrenched without warning at your throat and lungs. Sammy and I loved it, of course. It was something new, dramatic, part of the London experience.

After a day or so it was abating. Everything was still yellow-grey and hazy, but life in the city was returning to normal. In the early afternoon Sammy decided she'd had enough of reading for one day and that she would go back to Hammersmith.

She was walking around Russell Square towards the Tube station. A broad pale light, not sunlight exactly, but an attenuated beam from up there where the sun ought to be, came down over the square, promising that by tomorrow the smog would be gone. And in this momentary illumination, there he was! On the pavement outside 24 Russell Square a man in an overcoat and hat was hailing a taxi in an unmistakable voice – the voice she'd heard, on radio and recordings, reading, "April is the cruellest month, breeding / Lilacs out of the dead land". It was T. S. Eliot! It was the Master!

Sammy veered towards him, plunging her hand into her bag, feeling for the copy of that review, and saying, "Oh Mr Eliot. Excuse me."

He looked appalled, stricken, and she felt, seeing the fright in his eyes, a twinge of pity.

She didn't know then, but later discovered, that Eliot had spent many years hiding and escaping from his first wife, Vivien, from whom he had run away in the 1930s. Secretaries had protected him from her. He had come and gone by back doors. His address and phone number had been guarded from all but a very few close friends and associates. He would run from her in the street. And long after her death, an unexpected female voice calling to him in a public place could cause him to panic.

He was, in any case, a very shy and private man, and Sam could see that he would have done almost anything to escape. But he'd hailed the taxi, it was caught in the slow-moving traffic, threading its way across to him. He was trapped.

Now was Sammy's moment to say her piece. But her hand had closed, not on the sheet on which the offending review had been copied, but on her copy of his *Selected Essays*. As she pulled the much-thumbed book out of her bag she heard herself saying, "Would you sign this for me, please? I'm a great admirer of your work. Especially *The Waste Land*."

"Very kind," Eliot mumbled. "Most kind."

Sammy handed him the book and he wrote "T. S. Eliot" –

nothing more. At once he turned away, gave his instructions into the taxi which had now reached the curb, climbed in, and was gone.

Sammy looked at the signature. It was elegant, and she would keep it for ever – at the top left of the page her name in her own writing, "S. K. Conlan"; at the bottom right his, "T. S. Eliot".

She watched the taxi as it vanished into the dissipating fog on Southampton Row. Was she annoyed with herself for failing to challenge him, accuse him, demand he explain? Yes, she decided, she was; but also no, how could she be? She had T. S. Eliot's signature, proof for ever and ever that she'd seen him, spoken to him, that he'd been an arm's length from her. For just this moment – and it was a long one, never to be recalled without a renewal of pleasure – Sammy Conlan was overjoyed.

SIX

Jack and Jill

THERE IS A DREAM I'VE HAD AT WIDELY-SPACED INTERVALS over the years which harks back to my childhood in the suburb of Mt Eden when it was my job to see that our domestic fowls – "the chooks" – were fed morning and night, and that their water pail was clean and full. They were kept in two chicken-wire yards at right angles one to the other and divided by their hen house, so they could go from one yard, through their "house", and into the other; and these two yards, in turn, formed one corner of my father's vegetable garden which was in a hollow, part natural enclosure, partly enclosed by rock walls my grandfather had made when he built our house on the adjoining section. You went through a gate and down a path, past fruit trees, into "the lower garden" as it was called. There was a compost corner, an asparagus bed, the largest lemon tree I have ever known – so large I could climb into it – and the two fowl yards; and then the usual vegetable garden rows, peas, beans, silver beet, lettuces, carrots, whatever, often with lines of cotton and shreds of rag to keep the birds away.

Each day I went down with the chooks' food and climbed back with the pail, which I scrubbed and filled at the garden tap on the front lawn.

At odd times of the year when the ground was lying fallow and there were no crops to be protected, the fowls were allowed out of their yards, which they had beaten and scratched until nothing grew, to range free eating anything in the garden, plant or insect, that took their fancy. Though outside the wire, they were still in the enclosure of the lower garden, and since one wing was always clipped, couldn't fly away.

In the dream, which always seems to be in the present, I realize that a very long time has passed since I fed or watered the chooks. I'm stricken with anxiety and remorse and go at once through the gate, down past the fruit trees, along the path between the rows of vegetables, and to the gate of the yard, expecting to find them dead. I find the water pail is empty but the gate is open, and the hens are ranging free in my father's garden, which I now see is uncared for and has all gone to seed. Amazingly, though neglected all this time – many years – the birds have survived and are well. I fill the water pail and feed them. The relief is enormous.

This dream usually signals the onset of a new book. There is anxiety and relief; there is pleasure (the lower garden is a hidden, orderly, green and fertile place, even beautiful, with rich volcanic soil and a dark loamy smell); but there is also an inexplicable sadness, only ever to be assuaged by words on a page.

In the week after the evening of our meeting with Otto Stiltz and our meal at Mission Bay, that dream came to me twice.

Later again, having begun to write my new book, some vital element – confidence, energy, or something more mysterious – was lost, and I stopped. Once again my thoughts strayed to those alternative lives that perhaps still beckoned. The kitset house. The cycle tour through New Zealand. The movie-fest. The bibulous rustication in France. I became listlessly contented, contentedly listless. Why go on? It was such an effort, and who was listening? Sleep was such a pleasure.

Then, after a week or ten days of inaction, it came again – the dream – and I woke from it thinking of Sammy. When I went to my word processor that morning I sat a moment, remembering exactly, hearing it in my head, the particular clank made by the handle of that half-a-century-ago water pail, and seeing the texture of its inside surface which I used to clean with a brush kept by the garden tap on the front lawn. When scrubbed clean it had, not the look of polished steel or chrome, but a rough pale silver-grey brightness, almost white, with small flecks of black, a shine that was without any reflection.

I began writing. I could hardly keep up with the flow of ideas and the words that carried them. When I stopped for lunch I had written what would normally have been two or three days' work. After lunch I slept an hour or more, and didn't dream. When I woke, Louise was standing in the middle of the room looking down at me. "You're writing again," she said. "That's good."

"How did you know?"

She shook her head and pulled a French face. "I knew."
Later it occurred to me to wonder how she'd known I had stopped.

It must have been nine months or a year after the *Orsova* delivered Sammy and Rajiv and me to Tilbury Docks that the *Oronsay*, *Orsova*'s sister ship in the P&O fleet, arrived with

Friedrich Goldstein, his wife Ruth and their child Meir. They, however, were landed at Southampton.

Freddy and Sam had been writing to one another, and she knew exactly when and where he was arriving. She wanted to meet him, but he'd made it clear he didn't want that. She should stay away. He would get in touch with her as soon as he was settled and it was safe.

BE PATIENT, *PLEASE*, he begged; and although the parts of his letter she was reading to me didn't include those words, I could hardly miss their big letters, upside down across the coffee table.

What I couldn't be sure of was Freddy's attitude to Sam. I was much more suspicious and distrustful of him than she was, but when I showed any sign of my doubts Sammy dismissed them.

"You're just jealous, Laszlo," she said.

I didn't think she meant this literally, but perhaps she did. I talked a lot about Margot Derry at that time, but I thought much more about Sam. Margot was in Oxford. Sam was right there with me, in sight and in reach, day after day. When she wasn't there I was always looking around to see if she'd come in, wondering where she might be and what her absence might signify.

Sam also talked a lot about Margot. I thought it was a marking of boundaries. She and Freddy were one item; I and Margot could be another. But there was something in it that was ambiguous, contradictory. She talked about Margot too much, teased too often, asked too many questions.

Sammy and I had grown very close, but almost without noticing. The first time I remember her clearly was when the *Orsova* docked at Melbourne and everyone went ashore. In the old National Gallery of Victoria she and I were standing side by side in front of a major Renaissance painting, one of the first I'd ever seen. We recognized one another as fellow-passengers and talked about the painting. We had coffee together and shopped (or in my case window-shopped) our way back towards the ship.

Somewhere between Adelaide and Fremantle, in the Great Australian Bight, the ship ran into storms. Despite its much publicised "stabilizers" and its "28 000 tons and 25 knot speed", the *Orsova* heaved end to end and rolled side to side. I was not a good sailor and Sam, who did much better, and managed to eat and keep her meals down, was kind, even anxious about me.

After that, as we sailed into the calm of the middle latitudes, it seemed we'd become friends. When the temperatures rose and the lower cabins became insufferable at night, we took our bedding up on to the deck and slept there, side by side, with dozens of other young travellers. We played chess and table tennis, swam, drank at the bar, danced in the evenings. We arranged to be seated at the same table.

But even as early as Melbourne, the evening after we'd returned from our trip ashore, I'd been told about Freddy Goldstein. Right from the beginning that barrier was put between us.

So yes, I was jealous of him. I gave him serious thought, and it seemed to me there were two ways of interpreting his behaviour. The first was Sammy's view, which accepted his own account of himself. As she saw it Freddy was in love with her, but his Jewish wife, his commitment as a Jew to that marriage, the fact that they had a child and that Freddy himself was a child survivor of the Holocaust, made it impossible for him to do other than keep his affair secret, suffer the pain of it, and accept that sooner or later it must come to an end. All this he had put to her on a trip they'd made together to Canberra. She hated hearing it, but she accepted it. She couldn't help hanging on and hoping against hope; but she was a realist. Friedrich Goldstein, she believed, had History riding on his back. He was not a free man.

The alternative view – one I kept pretty much to myself, because even to hint at it produced an instant rebuff from Sam – was that Freddy had found himself deeper in with her than he'd meant to be, and was trying to extricate himself without hurting her so badly she would make a huge fuss, give the game away, "cause trouble". He was being gentle because he was afraid of the consequences of being tough. He'd seen his resignation in Sydney, and the plan to go to London and find work there, as an escape; but he'd been obliged to give ample notice, and to wait while he earned enough to pay for the journey. Meanwhile Sammy, not wanting to imitate Christina Stead's lovelorn heroine limping to England in her lover's wake, and having rich parents to call upon for the fare and for support, had pre-empted him by getting there first. Now he was once again going to have to placate her, keep her quiet while he slowly disengaged.

In this view, History was not so much a burden to Freddy Goldstein as an aid. Jewishness and the Holocaust had become for him a convenient excuse.

But these were not absolute alternatives – I knew that. Elements of both, true love and calculation, probably went into the making of his behaviour. And there would have been, in addition, inconsistencies, irresolution, contradictions – in the morning wanting one thing, and determining to have it; in the afternoon a change of heart, and a change of mind. Whichever way I looked at it, I never doubted that Freddy Goldstein must have been suffering.

Around this time Sammy talked of buying a car. I encouraged it, saying we would be able to get out of London and see something of the English countryside. I was already experiencing that "Londoned-out" feeling, a mixture of deprivation of the senses and over-stimulation of the nerves that invades most people who are not Londoners, those of us from the Southern Hemisphere especially, and especially during the English winter. But I was also thinking of Margot Derry in Oxford. I had no invitation to visit her, and to go alone might have been to invite a rebuff. But Sammy and I could go together. We could let Margot know we were coming, have tea together or go to a pub, ask her to show us her College, and then, as a *quid pro quo*, offer to take her for a drive. It wasn't much, but it might be a start.

Sometimes Sammy decided she would buy a car, other times that she didn't need it, that it would be a waste of her precious allowance. Then all at once, and without consulting anyone but a car salesman, she bought a Ford Popular. It was Freddy's imminent arrival that precipitated the decision. Our first trip, she decided (and already she'd developed a certain confidence – not misplaced – in making decisions for me) would be to Southampton where, if we could do it without being observed, we would watch him disembark.

The Ford was a new car and cost her £450 – next-to-nothing in new-century money, but that was the (not ungenerous) amount of my annual income on the scholarship. Registered 476AHY, it was tall-and-small, battleship-grey, narrow, basic inside, with a long gear-lever like a knob-topped walking stick, small bucket seats at the front, cramped double seat behind, and a boot which held the spare wheel with space for not more than one modest suitcase. Its tyres were narrow, its springs were not supple, it roared and shuddered if pushed much above fifty and felt unstable at that speed, as if it might topple cornering, or when the wind blew too hard. But a redoubtable car. We liked it, Sam and I, and even slept in it once or twice during a visit to the West Country, half-sitting up, half-lolling over, around and across one another. In a Ford Popular proximity was guaranteed, sex impossible.

On that drive to Southampton everything seemed exaggerated, vivid, funny, sexy. It was an effect of the English countryside, which we were seeing close up for the first time. We'd both been readers from an early age, and most of the books and poems and stories had been British. Neither of us had quite got used to the fact that we were in "England"; that what had existed for us only in books was now all around us, able to be seen and touched. We were colonials who had gone through the looking glass and were now truly on the other side. The unreal had become real, but without quite losing its unreality.

There's a sense in which it's true to say that only the natives can know their own country; and there's another sense in which only a foreigner who has apprehended it in words and in childhood can *recognize* it. It wasn't just the famous London landmarks, and not just the less spectacular but distinctly English things – red pillar boxes, comic policemen's helmets, bowler hats with rolled umbrellas – that we'd responded to since arriving. There had been endless smaller shocks of recognition. We were forever finding ourselves in

74

a scene from literature. And now, motoring through the green countryside, reading maps, detouring on back roads, we were experiencing it all over again. Here was "England" once more – that book world of woods, pasture, crop fields, water meadows; of lone cottages and small villages, orchards, hedgerows and haystacks; of a white pub, once a mill, with ancient black beams and thatched roof, backing on to a fast-running stream with a weir and mill-race; of a railway cutting smothered in wild flowers; of a farmer, wearing tweed jacket and tie, beating a single huge black-and-white cow along an empty, dung- spattered lane.

We sang, we chanted poems, we made weak jokes that seemed, not witty (they weren't) but so funny Sam had to pull over until the latest gale was past. We were drunk with it, released from the prison of London into "this earth of majesty, this seat of Mars / This demi-paradise, this other Eden."

Mid-morning and ahead of schedule, we parked, walked through some woodsy grassland, and climbed through trees towards the top of a small hill (all hills in southern England, we were finding, were small) from which we thought there might be views over the surrounding countryside. It was a warm, late spring day, no one about. The undergrowth and fallen branches were making it heavier going than we'd expected. Sammy was a pace or two ahead of me when she tripped and fell into thick soft grass, rolling sideways down the slope which was quite steep at that point. As she fell she laughed and reached out for me to check her fall. I grabbed and went with her. We came to rest against a log, wrapped around one another, entangled in the grass.

Walking behind her I'd been admiring her shape. Now

75

I had her in my arms. We looked at one another, into one another's eyes. She'd gone very still. We were tasting one another's breath. It was one of those moments when, inexperienced and uncertain, the male asks himself, "Does this mean . . . ?" "Does she want . . . ?" "Should I try . . . ?" Many years later, looking back, he can say the answer should almost certainly have been, "Yes, to all of the above."

There had been moments like this before – one especially, at night, at the rail of the ship going through the Red Sea; but none so close, so intimate, so adventitious. But now there was a scuffling and flapping noise in the long grass nearby, breaking the stillness. Startled, we jerked away from one another and up, looking to see what was going on, who or what was near. Only two or three yards away a crow flapped desperately out of a tangle of long grass, its wings lifting it four or five feet into the air, and then failing. The big bird, stalled in its take-off, fell back and disappeared.

I scrambled up looking for it. I found it in the grass. It was dead.

Hard to believe it should have died right at that moment, right there in front of us. Sammy, beside me now, turned it over, spread one of the wings, touched the strong beak, the strong sharp claws. "It's dead. It really is."

It was not a good moment for Nature to be turning on a spectacular. I moved closer to Sam, wanting again, wanting her, not this interruption. But it was as if she'd taken this avian seizure as an omen, a warning. She was all at once brisk, throwing the crow aside, dusting down her blouse, pulling her skirt around. Her breasts were outlined clearly, the nipples standing out, as she pulled out pins and refixed her hair. I reached towards her, but she turned her shoulder – her arms still raised, one hand holding the hair in place, the other pushing in the pins – and slid deftly past me.

I stayed where I was, disappointed, thinking "Nothing will come of nothing," but taking control of myself. For just a moment she leaned back against me. She knew what I was feeling and was sorry. The silence lasted a few seconds. Then, "Eleven-thirty," she said in a voice that was not quite her own. "Cripes! We'd better scoot, Laz."

I turned, and we made our way down the hill, back to the road.

At Southampton there were two or three big wharf sheds, with mezzanine areas where visitors could look down and watch arriving or departing passengers being processed through customs and immigration. Sammy had been counting on this, knowing that from up there she could see without being seen. Below us people were still going through with luggage on carts and trolleys, and officials in uniform were talking to them, opening suitcases, chalking cases and boxes. But it was only a trickle, not a crowd; and since there were two passenger ships, docked one on either side of the sheds, it wasn't possible to be sure which these few were coming from.

British officials can sometimes display a peculiar stubborn unhelpfulness, almost indistinguishable from stupidity, and this was compounded by Sammy's unwillingness to accept that we'd arrived too late. We spent a lot of time trundling about the sheds asking questions and getting half-answers before we were quite sure that all passengers from the *Oronsay* had been processed and were gone.

By now it was late afternoon. That moment in the long

grass, the closeness to something I hadn't been sure I wanted and now knew I wanted and couldn't have, was still with me. So it was easy to pretend I shared her disappointment at not even catching a glimpse of Freddy Goldstein. We were glum together, though for different reasons.

We found a fish and chip shop not far from the wharves where you could eat at little tables with red and white check tablecloths, looking out, over the top of a white curtain-screen that came half way up the window, to the narrow cobbled street, the wharf-piles, the green water, the white screechy gulls. We agreed we'd come too far just to turn around and go back again. We would go looking for a movie, a Western. It was a taste, tending towards an addiction, which Rajiv and I had developed since arriving in England.

That evening in Southampton, however, Sam and I couldn't find one, nor anything else we wanted to see; and so, on the point of giving up, but reluctant just to head back to the city, we stumbled into a seedy little picture palace to see an Italian movie Sam chose because the director's name was Federico. If she couldn't have her New Zealand-German-Jewish Freddy, she said, an Italian would have to do.

The Federico, of whom neither of us had heard until that moment, was Fellini, and the movie was *Nights of Cabiria* with Julietta Massina in the role of the prostitute who finds the man she can love – her "miracle", as she calls him – and who in the end is robbed and cheated by him. "Kill me," she says. "I want you to kill me." But he doesn't kill her – just takes all her money and leaves her in the woods. And then there's a final encounter with a stranger who wishes her "*Buona sera*," and against all probability, slowly, to the accompaniment of Nino Rota's music, up it comes, that inno-cent lop-sided courageous smile of hers.

We came out of the movie house saying nothing, Sammy in serious tears. So many years later I can still conjure up an image of the carpark in which we'd left the Ford Popular. It had become a *Fellini* carpark – sordid-picturesque, ugly-beautiful, unforgettable.

We drove back late towards London, staring ahead, seeing only the road and the ragged road edges, the wildflowers, like everything else in England, closed for the night, and the drunken moths staggering home down the wrong road of the headlights' beams. We were cosy together, Sam's disap-pointment and anxiety at having missed Freddy mixing with the mood of the movie, while I adopted a tone that was discreetly consoling. It seemed a long way in the dark, and neither of us cared. It could have gone on and on.

But as we were coming in, at one or two in the morning, to the empty glaringly-lit outskirts of London – the outskirts of the outskirts – where rain was falling, I felt Sam's mood had changed. I think I'd dozed for a while, and when I woke she was sitting up straight, both hands gripping the wheel.

I'd reached a point with Sam where I often felt I could "read" her by the way she behaved. At this moment, I decided, she'd been doing some serious thinking. She'd decided that she and I had come too close, and she was in a mood to reproach herself and put me in my place.

"What is it?" I asked. "Are you cold?"

She shook her head, staring into the streaky shower. After a few moments she said, "This morning, when we stopped and climbed that hill . . . When the bird . . . the crow . . ."

"Fell down dead. Yes?"

"If we'd . . . You know."

"Fucked?" That was daring. This was still the 1950s and the f-word wasn't said man to woman; only man to man. But she accepted it.

"I would probably have hated you."

So my "reading" had been right. I asked, "Hated it, or hated me?"

She was surprised by that. It took her a moment to answer: "Hated you, Laz."

"Afterwards?"

"I think so. Yes."

"So you might have hated me because you'd enjoyed it."

"I wouldn't have enjoyed it."

"Thank you for that," I said. I felt we were on the brink of our first quarrel, and perversely I was glad. It seemed to signal a new closeness.

"Don't take offence," she said. "I'm just trying to explain."

"If your explanation gives offence," I said, "offence will be taken."

"But Laszlo . . ." The tone asked for understanding. "You know what I mean, don't you?"

"Yes, you mean you might have been unfaithful to Freddy, and you think I should share your concern. Well I'm sorry, but I don't."

"I'm not going to let it happen."

"Fine. Nothing more to be said. I'm not a rapist."

"No of course not." She took a hand off the wheel and patted my sleeve. "Laszlo I'm sorry, I . . ."

"Would it have been so terrible?"

"Yes it would." She thought about it and decided to repeat it. "It *would*."

80

"He has a wife, hasn't he?"

"He can't help that."

Did she know how weak that sounded? I thought she must have, and let silence speak for me.

SEVEN

The Goldstein Story

AFTER THAT FIRST MEETING AT THE STUDENT UNION AND their walk to the bookshop in Glebe, Friedrich Goldstein had come after Sammy in a big way. Phone calls, messages, meetings in bookshops and coffee shops, even flowers. She'd held him at arm's length. He was a married man, five or six years her senior. She was young, inexperienced, a virgin, and afraid of what she might be getting in to. But the arm's length stuff had been half-hearted. She wanted Freddy; and once she'd had him she wanted more – wanted him exclusively.

So what she later came to recognize as a common pattern in such married-man unmarried-woman love affairs – "so common", she said to me once, "it's painful to think about" – was also the pattern of theirs. fter her initial resistance, quickly broken down, there was a period when their wants seemed to match, a few weeks, even months, but timeless and unforgettable, of secret meetings, passionate moments, strange beds, snatched opportunities. Of physical excess. Of (for her – and she thought also for him) true love truly satisfied.

Then, as her passion was released and she gave herself up to it, and as, correspondingly, the demands she made were greater, Freddy began to draw back. He wanted her, but not at the expense of an orderly life. He loved her, yes, but together

82

with a wife also loved, not in place of the wife. The obstacles which Sam had at first made much of, and which he had discounted, he now began to mention as if she had never heard or thought of them. He was a husband, a father, a Jew, a survivor. Not a survivor of the camps. But one who had been destined for death there, and had escaped it by a combination of luck and good management. That left him with an obligation. "Hitler made me a Jew," he told her.

"What does that mean?" she asked. "You're a Jew. So what?"

"It means," he replied, "that I'm not a free man."

Sammy didn't listen. It was noise, distracting, and she shut it out. She knew he loved her and told herself love would prevail. She was an optimist. She trusted to time. She trusted Friedrich Goldstein.

He had promised he would take her with him on an assignment to Canberra, but as the day approached she could see – but didn't want to see – that he was becoming anxious, regretting he'd ever mentioned it. Was she sure she wanted to come? He would be working most of the time. Canberra was an awful place . . .

Sam wasn't going to be put off, didn't even allow herself to believe that that was what he was trying to do. So they went and he was restless, uneasy, guilty, afraid he might be seen with her by someone who could "report back". There were some good meals, places of interest, busy love-making; there were a few moments of ecstasy, a great many tears, some bad quarrels and unspeakable glooms. And Canberra of the 1950s was indeed an awful place. On that, at least, Freddy had been right. Populated by civil servants, a city planned to make a statement, it struck them both as an imitation of an imitation, its spaces over-planned and under-occupied, with no history, no natural economy, nothing but politics and gossip to engage the mind. It was here, in this contrived wasteland capital, that Freddy, badgered by Sam's commanding love and unable any longer to meet it full-on, told her the truth: he would never – couldn't ever – leave his Jewish wife and child.

It was brave of him, she afterwards thought. At the time she found it hurtful, hateful, cruel, unnecessary – as if he had dragged her off to this nightmare place in order to shoot her dead. "Why don't you do it?" she railed at him. "Kill me and be done with it?" (No wonder she wept, a year later, at Julietta Massina's Cabiria.)

He sighed and held his head in his hands. This was his "Jewish despair posture" she told him. But what about *her*? What about *her* despair. Being a Jew didn't give him exclusive rights on pain and suffering. "What did you get me into this for? And why drag me all the way to Canberra just to tell me you've had enough?"

But he hadn't had enough. That wasn't the message. It was just that there were limits . . .

"Oh yes limits," she said. "How convenient."

They were parked, as Sam afterwards remembered it, in Freddy's Holden (it was new – Australia's first home-made car) on a long concrete bridge with a concrete strip of highway stretching in either direction, the bridge itself spanning a man-made "lake", yet to be filled with water. The sun was going down. There was a line of gum trees, bark hanging off them like soiled bandages, their top branches leafless sticks; there was some desolate, wire-enclosed parkland with wallabies standing about like movie extras waiting for shooting to begin; there was the usual insane kookaburra laughter dying in the distance, and up close the zoom of cars up and down the concrete strip in ones and twos, making the relative quiet between seem more than ever empty and bleak.

They argued inside the Holden, outside it on the walkway, inside it again. They drove along the road, out of town, stopped to argue, drove back towards town and stopped once more. She got out of the car and ran away from him, back along the road to nowhere, knowing he would have to come after her and that when he did she, lacking the means to get back to Sydney, would have to get in with him again.

She said every hard thing she could think of and Freddy replied almost – though perhaps more delicately – in kind. She ranted. She wept for herself. He wept and she stopped weeping for herself and wept because he was weeping.

When there was nothing bad left to say, they made it up, and made love, in the car first (the sun had gone now) and then back at their motel. But what had been said was there between them, a sadness, an obstacle.

Exhausted equally by the quarrel and the "making it up", they lay side by side, two stone figures on a tomb, naked, her right hand in his left, both staring at the ceiling from which, she noticed, the paint that looked fresh and bright and recent was threatening to unroll like a badly fixed sheet of paper.

"You're my Latvian flower-seller," Freddy said.

On the brink of dozing, she couldn't speak; could only respond with a barely audible "Mmmmmm," its questioning inflection inviting him to explain, but not insisting on it.

"It's called the sin of the father," he said.

And then they slept. But later, eating in a restaurant close to the Parliament, she remembered it, and asked what he'd meant.

Paul Goldstein, Friedrich's father, was born 1898 in Berlin of a liberal Jewish family who for several generations had been Germans quite as much as they were Jews, and would have continued to be if the times had permitted. The synagogue was there, and the rabbi, and the relatives' weddings and bar mitzvah and funerals. If they didn't eat pork it was because they never had eaten it, not because they thought that it mattered very much. If the boys were circumcised it was because it was a tradition, and it would have been embarrassing to be different. They were part of the Jewish community, with its varying levels of "observing". But they were equally a part of the community at large – cheerful, prosperous, patriotic Germans who gave one another presents at Christmas, and among whom Paul was the glum exception, sometimes known as Cassandra.

A brilliant student, highly successful in his medical studies, Paul was renowned for predicting bad outcomes. "There he goes again," his family would say. But they would have done well to look more closely at the myth they invoked when they teased him. Paul would prove to be Cassandra indeed: right in his dire forecast for the family, and not listened to.

Sibling loyalty and German patriotism had combined to persuade him to follow his older brother Klaus enlisting in the army for the War of 1914. He had done what was required of him in that conflict and survived unscathed. Klaus also came back alive, but wounded. Shrapnel had blasted his upper right arm, shredding muscle, destroying nerves, shattering bone. His recovery was slow, took many months, and at the end of it the arm was withered, the hand almost paralysed. Klaus, who had earned the Iron Cross (second class) for the action in which he was wounded, cheerfully called himself "second class Klaus" and set about learning to use his left hand. But then, very slowly, movement came back into the fingers of the right. The movements were slow and stiff, and the hand itself looked strange – pink in colour and white when touched.

It was Paul, the younger son, who married first. The family made no complaint that blonde blue-eyed Hilde Voigt was not Jewish; but Hilde's family could not quite hide their disappointment that Paul was.

The war left Germany's economy in a state of near-collapse, and in the decade which followed, the Goldstein jewellery business struggled, seemed at times close to ruin, but survived. As the numbers of the unemployed rose towards three million, the Goldsteins continued, though not to prosper, at least to hold their own.

But now, as the Nazis began to gain a significant following, vowing to rid Germany of the Jews who were polluting its Aryan purity and stealing its wealth, Paul believed they should be taken at their word. While his family told him that they couldn't mean what they said, and that even if they did, the German people would never let them do what they wanted to do, Paul talked about emigration, and began sending money, a little at a time, to bank accounts in Amsterdam and Milan.

It was during this period that the whole family took a holiday together on the Baltic, as they had done for many years. There was a favourite hotel, with sand dunes on one side, a pine plantation on the other, and the sea in front. They had always stayed there and believed they had a reservation for the first two weeks of every August. But this time they were refused rooms, and were forced to take lesser accommodation in a tavern a mile down the road.

Brooding on this, not accepting the comforting explanations which the rest of his family invented and exchanged, Paul was unreasonably troubled one day by the sight of two small boys and their sister, on the beach in front of the hotel the Goldsteins had thought of as "theirs", decorating a sand castle with small paper flags. They had dug a dungeon under the castle, barred with black sticks, and put behind the bars a lead toy man in a dark suit and black hat.

Stopping in his walk, gripped as if by a vision of what was to come, Paul asked the children, in a voice which even to himself sounded abrupt and harsh, "Is he a Jew?"

They looked at the man in the cage, and then back at Paul. What was the right answer? He'd taken them by surprise and they weren't sure.

"Yes," one boy said, and the other said, "No."

"I'm a Jew," Paul said. "Would you lock me up?"

They looked at him with blue, innocent eyes. The boys shook their heads. "No," they said; they wouldn't. And their little sister whispered it too. "No."

"For me you would make an exception?" Paul said, his voice rising angrily. "Why? Why would you? I don't believe you."

They drew back, alarmed. Paul saw himself in their eyes – a madman. "Never mind," he said. "All a mistake. Here . . ." He gave them each a few pfennigs. "Buy yourselves some toffee." And rushed on along the beach, blushing, feeling his shoes filling with sand.

As the election of 1932 approached there was an atmosphere of hysteria and violence. Nazi vilification of Jews
increased. Everywhere there were flags, banners, uniforms,
candlelit marches. Loudspeakers in the streets broadcast
speeches and slogans. Somehow the idea took hold that
Germany had reached its "moment of destiny" when a choice,
a commitment, had to be made: the hammer-and-sickle, or
the swastika. Rational voices said it didn't have to be either,
there was plenty of space in between those extremes; but
these were not times when rational voices were listened to.

It was a time of excitement as well as of fear. There was
heroic singing, much of it beautiful, but always with a note
of frenzy and an edge of violence. Not telling family or
friends, but wanting the experience and (as he put it to
himself) to "know the enemy", Paul went to a Nazi rally. He
saw the long banners and the brilliant columns of beamed
light, listened to the music of Wagner and the silence
which followed, felt the thrill as thousands of arms rose and
thousands of voices shouted in unison to greet the entrance
of Germany's future Führer. For just a moment, silent, but
in his head, Paul joined the mass. His arm remained at his
side, but he imagined it too was raised, that his voice was
shouting "Heil". Then he did raise them both, arm and voice,
but only so he would not attract attention. By now he was
back inside himself, acting a part, conscious of who and what
he was, and what the figure up there at the microphones,
voice cracking with emotion, hands clasping at the air in
front of him, was saying about race and blood. Paul's brother
had shed blood for Germany. It had been the wrong blood,
impure, *jüdisches Blut*. As in the Horst-Wessel song, soon to
be Germany's other national anthem, the blood of the Jew

was destined to spurt under the Nazi knife.

It was July when the election was held. Paul walked with Hilde, pushing the infant Friedrich in his pram, along the Unter den Linden where they sat for a time at a table outside one of the crowded cafés, strolled on, sat again. They watched the movement of summer light on the dusty lime trees, on the Kaiser's Palace, on the Brandenburg Gate. Paul took mental photographs of the whores in their bright dresses on Friedrichstrasse, and the soldiers in grey guarding the Tomb of the Unknown Soldier, saying inside his head with immense sadness, "All this is coming to an end". It was something he would remember long afterwards – the sense, like a last slow-motion moment before a crash, that what was about to happen was inevitable, and yet also (and contrarily) that it might have been avoided.

Early in 1933 Hitler became Reich Chancellor, and almost at once reports and rumours brought fear to the Goldsteins. Political organisations and trade unions were banned, newspapers shut down, books burned, informers encouraged, communists beaten up in the streets. Jews were dismissed from jobs, their shops and businesses picketed by Nazi storm troopers, or closed altogether. There was talk of "concentration camps" – places of brutality, deprivation, humiliation, where you would go hungry and might have to lick your meal off the floor to amuse a guard and escape a beating. New definitions of "treason" were added, new laws enacted, new restrictions placed on freedom. It was hard to see how it could go on, where it would end.

Apologists in the newspapers said Germans had only to point themselves the way the Führer intended the Reich to go and everyone could be part of a harmonious future. But the choice was available only to Aryans. If you were a Jew – if you had even one Jewish grandparent – you were excluded. You were not wanted. You were part of "the Jewish problem" yet to find its "final solution".

In September 1935 the Nürnberg laws were enacted "protecting German blood and German honour". There could be no new marriages between Jews and Aryan Germans, and sexual relations across the racial divide became illegal. The Goldstein parents, Joachim and Beatrice, were required to dismiss their housekeeper because she was female, Aryan, and under the age of forty-five. As a Jew Joachim could not be trusted to employ this flower of German womanhood, who might fall victim to his Semite lust. She, however, wept at the loss of a good employer and of a job.

When the Goldstein business was picketed, its doors and walls daubed with JUDE, Aryan neighbours were sympathetic, embarrassed by such attacks, but perhaps accepting (how could the Goldsteins know, one way or the other?) the general argument that Germany's economic ruin had it roots in "the Jewish problem".

"What is the Jewish problem?" Hilde asked a man who came to their door selling brooms and quoting Hitler.

"I'm not sure," the man said. "But I can tell you this. It's serious."

For the Goldsteins that sense of security which every human being thinks is "normal" until it goes, had vanished. Afraid of writing letters, of talking on the phone, of speaking their thoughts aloud on the streets, they talked only behind closed doors – of emigration, of what the future might hold for them if they stayed – and kept their voices down.

Paul, a hospital registrar, kept his job, at least for the time being. As in every work place, it became obligatory to meet one another in wards and corridors with the Nazi stiff-armed salute and the greeting "Heil Hitler". Many found this absurd, inconvenient, childish; but fear was beginning to affect everyone. No one spoke out against it. Soon they got used to it. Paul gave it grudgingly, mumbled "Heil Hitler", and hated himself.

There were new regulations making it illegal to send money abroad. Paul had his two foreign accounts and could find ways around the obstacles, though no longer lawfully. It was dangerous – the punishments were severe – but he took the risk. Now his father and brother were also fearful, but still persuaded themselves that things must soon begin to improve. Urged by Paul at least to prepare himself an escape route, Klaus listened but shook his head. He had married a distant relative, there was a young child and a second on the way, and the idea of emigration was something he couldn't face. Surely his war service and his Iron Cross would protect them.

"Don't you listen to what Hitler says?" Paul asked. "It's time for us to go."

Klaus shrugged it off with a joke. The play, he said, was getting too interesting for him to want to leave the theatre just yet. Neither of the brothers could have imagined what his role would be in the final act.

Paul was ready to go, and hesitated only because Hilde did not want to leave their homeland. And then something happened in the hospital which made him decide that they must.

An unconscious man was brought in by storm troopers. Paul, on duty, asked how the man had been injured. The SA officer explained that this was a known communist who had a hand-press hidden somewhere on which a banned news sheet, propagating "lies about the Reich", was being printed. The man had refused to admit this, or tell the authorities where the press was being kept.

"But it was found?" Paul asked.

No, the trooper said. That was the problem.

"So how do you know it exists?" Paul asked.

"We have been informed."

"What if your informer was lying?"

Now the officer turned cold, threatening eyes on him. "What reason," he asked, "would a loyal citizen of the Reich have to lie to us?"

When they had gone and the injured man was stripped and examined it was found he had been severely beaten. Apart from the head injury, which was serious, he had a damaged eye, broken jaw, nose, and probably ribs, and bruising, cuts and abrasions all over his body. Paul noted also that he was circumcised.

In the night, when Paul was off duty, the man died from the damage to his brain. By morning a post-mortem report had been prepared. It gave the cause of death as dysentery.

A few days later, still upset by what had happened, Paul came up out of the Berlin Underground into a crowded square and found himself only a short distance from where Dr Goebbels, the Nazi propaganda chief, was reaching the frenzied climax of a speech about how Germany's agony would be over once the Jewish problem was sorted out. "If time proves me wrong," he shouted, "you can call me a lunatic."

Without thought, and before the applause had time to crank itself up, Paul found himself shouting, "YOU *ARE* A LUNATIC."

All eyes turned on him. On the other side of the crowd he saw Brown-shirts moving towards him, breaking into a run. He turned and ran back into the Underground and by good luck found a train standing in the platform, its doors just closing. He dived in and they shut behind him. Sweating, cursing his own folly, he jumped out at the next stop, ran to another platform, and jumped on the first train that came in. He had done this two or three times and travelled many miles before he stopped to see where he was. He didn't recognize the name of the station. I don't know where I am he thought. His next thought was, If I don't know where I am, neither do they. And he stopped running.

But that was the trigger. A few weeks later he was in Amsterdam with Hilde and little Friedrich. From there they travelled by circuitous routes, involving both sea and rail, to Palestine. It was a journey Freddy hardly remembered, except that his parents afterwards said they had kept running into obstacles, and had been hungry every day.

Paul had hoped to work as a doctor; but he had gone to Palestine knowing that it was full of well-qualified German-Jewish pessimists like himself. He was not surprised that he could find no employment in the medical field. It didn't matter. They had escaped. They were alive.

He sold herrings on the streets of Haifa, made a living, and was (for a gloomy man) almost cheerful. Even Freddy, though only an infant at the time, had recollections of that city – the heat of the sun, the pale crooked buildings, the crazy streets parting and joining but all sloping down towards a very blue sea; the bright colours of Arab washing hanging out to dry above ancient ruined battlements; the cool leafy courtyards; the scents of jasmine and narcissus, eucalypts and oranges; the market crowded with hooded Arabs and orthodox Jews; the laden donkeys driven by boys with sticks – and once, the tangy breath of a donkey as he, a very small child, looked up into its face.

Meanwhile Hilde's family, whose disapproval of her marriage had increased in proportion to the Nazi Party's hold on power, and who had not been forewarned of this escape to Palestine, wrote urging that it might be best for her and the child to come home. Perhaps she should think about the opportunity the Nazis offered Aryans to get an easy divorce from a Jewish spouse. As for the child, who was now, according to the new racial classification, a *Mischling* – the family had talked about it and offered a solution. Hilde could easily claim that little Friedrich, who took after his mother's family, not Paul's, was a "love child to an Aryan lover". Her brothers would back her up in this story, and even supply a voluntary "father" from among their friends. She could say that the truth had come out in Palestine and was the final cause of the break-up of the marriage. Even Paul, they suggested, if he had the welfare of his wife and child at heart, might agree that this would be for the best.

Hilde didn't show her husband the letter. She didn't reply and did her best to cast her family out of her thoughts.

Haifa was dirty, noisy, foreign; by the standards of their old life they were living in poverty. But there was beauty too, and excitement, especially for a young woman who had never travelled outside her homeland, and had never seen any other sea than the Baltic. There was a well-established German-speaking colony in the town, the Jews were good to one another when they weren't quarrelling, and Hilde thought of it, not as "for ever" but as "in the meantime", until Germany had rid itself of Hitler and his strutting, barking fanatics.

They lived with two other Jewish refugee families in a big half derelict house among pines high above the port. The wind sighed in the pines, which cooled and, together with the scent of cypresses, gave the house its faint but particular fragrance, while below and beyond, the Mediterranean spread itself out into a streaky, hazy distance that made of the colour blue a declaration, almost an active verb.

Paul liked Palestine, but felt uneasy (he was always uneasy) about its future as a homeland for Europe's Jews. The Jewish claim to this region might be ancient; but what could that possibly mean to Arabs who had occupied it for hundreds of years? To some it was an affront. Already there were militant groups on both sides preparing to fight, and sometimes reports of shootings and explosions.

Safety was what he wanted; security; distance from trouble. In the pocket Atlas he had brought with him he looked long and hard at New Zealand – a place so far you could go no further, but said to be civilized, already a refuge for some of his race.

But now Paul's "Latvian flower-seller" enters the story. Her name was Marthe Borowska. She was young, pretty, lively – "happy by temperament, sad by circumstance", as Paul later described her. She had come, a Jewish refugee from Riga, after the death of her husband in an outburst of political street violence which had become a small localized pogrom. Marthe had loved her husband. Unattached and lonely, she grieved for him. But she was a buoyant character and admitted that even in her grief she couldn't help responding to "sunshine, good bread and human company". Paul's herrings barrow was beside her flower stall. The door to the single room she rented on the waterfront was only yards away. He found her irresistible; she found him convenient. Soon they were lovers. "A man who smells of herrings," he said to Freddy in a rare moment of levity, "will not be suspected of smelling of sex."

In the weeks that followed Paul discovered something about himself which would afterwards remain mysterious and unexplored. He had heard of men whose infidelities were revealed because they lost interest in their wives. In his case it was quite otherwise. His passion for Hilde, and his desire for her, were refreshed and renewed. Marthe by day down at the harbour, Hilde by night up on the hill – they seemed each to shine, enriched by difference. Paul discovered new faith in himself, new strength. Not knowing why, Hilde liked him better, loved him more.

But his moods were always volatile. The "black dog" of his depression was never far away. To soar as high as he did during the time of his affair with the flower-seller meant a plunge would follow. When it came it took the convenient form of remorse. How could he have been unfaithful to Hilde whom he loved so much, and who had given up the security of her homeland and come with him to live in relative squalor among potential enemies?

"The old-time Jew came out in me," he told his son. "I beat my breast and tore my hair. I wanted to repent. Who is it says 'It is never possible to repent of love?' I couldn't repent, but I tortured myself with remorse."

The drama, the melodrama, of it all was too much for Marthe and she shut her door on him. "Go away," she told him, "and don't come back until you have regained your sanity. I love to have your juice on my sheets, but not if it means your tears on my pillow."

Paul didn't like that either – he wanted her still – but it seemed to make confession possible. To relieve himself he told Hilde what had happened, thinking that he would be forgiven, understood, even perhaps pitied. Hilde did not understand and certainly didn't pity. Her pain was immense, her actions full of grief and violence. She shouted, wept, showed him the letter from her family which previously she'd kept hidden. When he made excuses she flew into a violent rage, tore up photographs, broke plates and vases. "Get out," she told him. "Go, and don't come back."

He went. Both doors now – Hilde's and Marthe's – were shut on him.

He found aid and comfort, a bed and meals, in the household of a kindly Rabbi. But meanwhile Hilde was wasting no time. As an Aryan there were no obstacles to her return. She sent word to her family, packed, and prepared to go back to Germany with their son, determined to divorce.

But as she stood at the rail with their little boy, the ship casting off ready to sail out of that artificial harbour so recently constructed by the British, Hilde looked, first up at the evening light falling on Mount Carmel with its olive groves, its pines and cypresses, then down at the port area with its squalid and colourful markets and cafés, and recognized that she had loved this town and was going to miss its rich noisy clashing life.

And then, worse, she saw a familiar figure standing on the dock, staring up at her. He hadn't shaved, his hair was untidy and in need of cutting, his clothes were ragged. But what was hardest for her was his tragic face. It made her sad, and it made her angry that it made her sad. He was weak, a fool, a destroyer, she told herself, trying to fight down her pity.

So the two of them, Hilde and Paul, husband and wife, stared at one another through tears while the gap widened between ship and shore, and the dark came down.

EIGHT

Learning and Teaching

AFTER FRIEDRICH GOLDSTEIN ARRIVED IN LONDON THERE was a period when I didn't see much of Sam. This was partly, I supposed, because she was now seeing a good deal of Freddy; or at least making herself available to see him when that was possible. But also her circumstances changed in other ways. She left Castlenau Mansions and found a small flat for herself in Doughty Street. That too, I guessed, was so she would have somewhere to take Freddy when he was free. It was in walking distance of the British Museum; but now, with the cost of running a car, and always finding new and more expensive things to do in London, she was overspending her allowance and decided it was time for paid employment. So Rajiv and I could no longer count on seeing her at the Reading Room.

Between completing her degree in Sydney and boarding the *Orsova* Sammy had taken a course in shorthand typing. Now she registered with a "temping" agency. There was plenty of work, and at first she chose short-term jobs – an advertising agency, a solicitor's office, a trade journal, a job with the Dean of St Paul's.

Then came her three-day-a-week job with Marx MacLaren, literary editor of a famous weekly. Sam took shorthand, typed letters, kept the files, made tea, emptied wastepaper baskets, ran out to clear the Post Office box or to buy milk, sandwiches, cigarettes. As well as a shorthand typist she was the office dogsbody, the girl Friday, and she loved it. Famous writers came and went. (On her first day Evelyn Waugh showed her his newly monogrammed gold cuff-links.) She was picking up gossip about the literary world – who had a mistress (or two mistresses), a mad wife, a homosexual lover, an alcohol problem. It was, she said, as if she'd stopped writing her *Secret History of Modernism* and started to live it.

The office where the literary part of the paper – its back pages – was produced was a single big room, Marx MacLaren sitting at a desk with a naked light suspended over his head and windows directly behind, so it was difficult to see his expression. At a desk to one side of him sat his deputy, Wilma Marienbad, a small woman with the features of a pretty mouse, who never went out to lunch but kept supplies of nuts, chocolate, dried fruit and biscuits in her top drawer and used to half turn away from her boss and nibble discreetly. On the other side was another woman, Teresa Foot, Marx MacLaren's assistant. These three, God and his handmaidens Sammy called them, faced down the room in which all the other desks and tables and filing cabinets were arranged so Marx (who moved so little and was so pale Sam thought of him as a corpse) could see what was going on and give instructions without getting up or using the phone.

Sam told me about her interview for the job She was directed to a little side office kept for such occasions. When she went in Marx MacLaren was sitting at a desk copy-editing a typescript. He glanced up, nodded her to a chair, and went on working. Time passed – she thought twenty minutes at least, and probably half an hour. It seemed a deliberate rudeness, and she would have got up and left except that she couldn't think why he would bother to be rude to an unknown "temp". There had to be some other explanation. That he was absorbed in his work? But why here and now, with an audience of one?

She was still puzzling over this when he made the last correction, screwed the top on his fountain pen and looked up. For a few moments he stared at her, saying nothing. It was what she called "a fact-gathering stare" – nothing sexual about it, nothing improper. "You're from Australia," he said.

She said she was. He remarked that it was a long way to have come. "I'm from Scotland," he said.

Sam nodded and said, "I've heard."

"What have you heard?" he asked, suspicious.

"That you're from Scotland."

"That's right. I am." He looked truculent now. Defiant. Once again she was puzzled. He shuffled his papers together. "So . . . Is there anything you want to ask?"

There wasn't, and the job was hers.

All her dealings with Marx were like that. She was sometimes offended by him, and almost always puzzled, and yet she liked him. He was amusing – "mordant" was the word she used. He disliked what he called "sneering", and yet he was himself a prodigious sneerer. He barked at his staff, was edgy, and often angry. But when, a few days after she started there, he made Sam burst into tears (things weren't going well with Freddy and her nerves were frayed) Marx MacLaren was disconcerted, insisted on making her a cup of tea, called her "Lassie" and patted her hand.

Later, when he took her on full time, he said something that made her think he meant to take her to lunch. Instead, he brought two pork pies to the little side office, with paper plates, plastic knives and forks, and two sachets of tomato sauce. They ate together largely in silence. "Did you like the pie, Sammy?" he asked when they'd finished.

She said she'd liked it very much.

Marx nodded. "Guid. So you can start full time on Monday then."

On the rare occasions when I called for Sam at the office Marx and his principal retainers on either side would glance up, register with relief that I was not someone whose presence needed to be acknowledged, and go on working. There were few greetings, a minimum of charm in that place; but the literary pages it produced were famous.

Between Sam and me there was still a bond, but it had changed, and I thought this could only be because she and Freddy Goldstein were lovers again. I told myself I should have been pleased – pleased for her, but of course I wasn't. Freddy had always been an invisible door between us. Now I felt the door was shut. No more lyrical moments; no more dreamy night walks by the river. We were still friends, but brotherly and sisterly; and I remember saying to her once, hearing on her radio the Johann Strauss song "Brüderlein und Schwesterlein", "Darling, they're playing our song!" It was either a joke she didn't "get", or one she didn't like, because she looked at me blankly and didn't laugh.

Days, perhaps even weeks, went by when we didn't see one another. I missed her, and noticed myself noticing other young women. One I noticed in particular was Heather on the landing – Miss Tina of AWAYCARE. From time to time I would knock at her door and say she was wanted on the phone. "It's the shop," I would say, repeating the baritone woman's message.

"The shop? Oh yes, ta, Laszlo. Thanks." Heather would blunder past me, pushing back her hair and bumping into walls. These brief exchanges were anything but impersonal. We were terribly aware of one another, and shy.

One day, heading home, I found myself standing beside her in the street outside the Kensington High Street tube station, waiting to cross at the lights. It was raining, there were gusts of wind, and she was trying to hold up an umbrella in one hand and in the other a cake box hanging on a strip of ribbon, while keeping a newspaper clamped under one arm. I offered to help. She said, "You could hold the cake. Or . . . No, you're getting wet. Let's do it this way." She took back the cake and gave me the umbrella. "You're tall," she said.

We walked along, keeping close under the umbrella which was small, frilly and ineffective. When we got to our entrance in Phillimore Gardens and went in, she said she would bring me a slice of the cake. Someone at the shop had had a birthday, the manager had bought a big cake, and they'd "whacked it up, fair shares all round".

As she told me this she blushed, as if she regretted introducing that fictional "shop". But later she brought me a slice of the cake, and although she declined my invitation to come in and share it with me, saying she'd already eaten all she could manage, the ice had been broken between us and from then on, meeting on the landing, on the stairs, in the hallway, in the "area" where the rubbish bins were kept, we always stopped to talk. One morning, picking up mail from the table in the hallway, she asked about my friend, the Australian girl – she thought she'd heard me call her

"Sammy". Heather hadn't seen her for a while . . .

I explained that Sammy had a job now on a literary paper. As we walked up the stairs together I pointed out the "MR. SPITFIRE" card she'd pinned on Mr Spiteri's door, and told Heather the name she'd invented for Harry Pulsford. I said too much too fast.

"She looks clever," Heather said, with smiling eyes. "She's your girlfriend, is she?"

I explained about Friedrich Goldstein and she said, "So she's not your girlfriend, but you'd like her to be."

Heather's personality was vivid, easy, open. She was pretty and shapely, and when she smiled her face lit up – but almost too much, as if she couldn't quite control her features. The lips quivered and the teeth were uneven, making her seem vulnerable. And then there was the "shop", her secret, which could make her suddenly cagey and withdrawn.

I was a normal young man of my time, well-fed and hungry for sex of which very little was on offer, so my thoughts about Heather tended to be florid, and she, a professional, must have recognized this as surely as a motor mechanic recognizes, when he glances under the bonnet of a car, that the engine is overheating.

Soon we were familiar enough to step into one another's rooms. There was only one armchair in my bedsit, and not a lot of space. When I insisted she take the chair while I sat on the edge of the bed, it meant we had to angle our thighs like the sides of a parallelogram, and from time to time flanks would touch. Proximity – *almost* touching like that – I found distracting, so next time I let her take the bed while I sat in the chair. She chose not to sit with her feet on the floor – probably the bed was too high – but took her shoes off and sat with legs curled under. It meant the skirt was pulled up and there was a lot of leg, and some dark places under-and-between, right there in front of me. I'm sure she was amused by the circuitous flight-path my eyes took, passing from her face to a book we were discussing, or to my mug of tea, and back again, without overflying any of the perilous regions of her lower body.

Heather asked me what I was studying. At first I answered in a brief and unsatisfactory way. She bridled, thinking I thought her too stupid, or too uneducated, to understand, but it was not that at all – as I explained. Really it was because I thought she – or anyone not, so to speak, "in the game" – would find it boring.

I remember that open smile of hers as she said, "Try me."

Right at that time I was having problems getting my supervisor to agree to the line of approach I wanted to take to my studies in Shakespearean drama. The conventional critical approach of the time irritated me. It tended to be moralistic, as if England's greatest poet had set out only to teach us how to behave; but when I read the plays – and this was where my supervisor and I couldn't agree – I was always struck by a feeling that they were morally neutral. I don't mean that there weren't some notable villains and some unambiguously "good" characters: of course there were. But I saw these just as the facts of the *story*. They were data, white stones and black stones, not illustrations in a good behaviour manual. I was (I now see) thinking like a writer, a "teller of tales". I wanted to get away from moralising and think about the practical side of Shakespeare's work.

To persuade my supervisor to let me take this approach was difficult. How would I go about it, he wanted to know. What would I write about? So I'd offered him an example, and I now put it to Heather. I said it had struck me that Shakespeare could not have dreamed up two such dominating and violent middle-aged women as Volumnia in *Coriolanus*, and Lady Macbeth, unless there had been one very unusual senior boy actor (women were not allowed on the stage and female characters had to be played by boys) to fill those roles; or maybe, more than a boy, a man (had anyone thought of *that*?) – the Elizabethan equivalent of a drag queen! A boy/man or man/woman with a big voice and a big personality, capable of dominating, by strength of character as Volumnia dominates her warrior son, and by sexual presence as Cleopatra dominates Antony. Someone, after all, had to play these parts, it had to be a male, and Shakespeare had to have thought about it before writing the play.

That was just one example. In fact I wanted to look into every known detail of Shakespeare's professional life – theatres, actors and actors' companies, relations with city authorities, aristocratic and royal patronage, the common people who came to cheer, the puritans who stayed away – and see how these various forces influenced his choices of plot, story, action, character.

My supervisor had objected, but in a rather feeble, hand-flapping way, as if he couldn't think of a reason but would let me know when one occurred to him. Heather saw the point at once. That's not surprising, you might think. In the full blast of my enthusiasm, politeness alone would have required one who was not an expert to pretend at least to interest, and why not (it would cost her nothing) agreement. But this was much more than politeness. Heather was excited. Her smile broke out. Her eyes shone. It was as if I had given her something – and I had: knowledge. She wanted to give me something in return, and what did she have to offer except what otherwise she sold at a price?

I have jumped ahead of myself with that sentence, but that is what it came to – slowly, over time. It was a trade. I would give her the contents of my mind; she, in return, would give me the use of her body. It happened step by step; but before the final step was taken, the one into bed, the facts of what she did for a living had to be broached.

We reached a point in our casual visits and conversations where I felt it was safe – or not, anyway, too much of a risk – to hand back to her the card she'd dropped on the stairs. There was a black and precarious silence, and then, as she looked hard at me and recognized that, far from disapproving, I was excited by what it revealed about her, she relaxed. Yes, she was a call girl. We talked about it, then and later. Her clientèle were businessmen away from their wives. Sheaths were the rule, so there was no danger of disease for either party. Mostly she had to fake pleasure because these men weren't good at talking to women – that's why they had to pay for female company. "Usually," she said, "there's nothing there. No feeling. No real closeness. It's mechanical."

Later, when we had become lovers, I reminded her of this and asked whether she faked it with me. "Well, do I?" she replied, and I didn't know. Later again I knew she didn't, and thought on those first occasions, when I was so much the beginner, she must have.

I remember the first time we fucked because it came out of an intellectual excitement – mine – which I somehow communicated, and which lit a fire in her. I had been reading Shakespeare's last four plays and was all at once struck by the strangeness of two characters in *The Winter's Tale*, Antigonus and Autolycus, opposite and parallel even to their nine-letter names beginning with A2-something-t" and ending with "u–s". Antigonus, a "good" man who does what he's told, is eaten by a bear. Autolycus, cheat, liar, thief and fraud, escapes punishment and lives.

Antigonus appears in the tragic first half of the play, Autolycus in the second, the comic part.

What had occurred to me was that when Shakespeare's company put the play on, the same actor might have played both roles, first one then the other. When the Clown, in a bit of black comedy, describes to the Shepherd how he has seen the bear eating his victim, he says, "And then . . . to see how the bear tore out his shoulder bone, how he cried to me for help and said that his name was Antigonus."

Sixteen years pass and the second half introduces Autolycus for the first time – picking the pocket of the same Clown while pretending he's been severely beaten by robbers. The Clown goes to help him up from the ground, and Autolycus howls, "O good sir, softly good sir! I fear, sir, my shoulder-blade is out!"

I imagined the actor – and it could even have been Shakespeare himself – winking to the groundlings, who would recognize this as the same man who played Antigonus, the character whose shoulder blade was torn out by the bear.

Heather liked this idea. My enthusiasm was contagious. She liked especially the thought of Shakespeare himself playing these two parts, one after the other. But she asked me to explain something. She could see that the parallel of the names, and the shoulder blades. But did I mean . . . Would

Shakespeare have *meant* something by this device? Would it have had a *point*?

I was pulled up short. I said first that I supposed yes, there had to be a point. Then I said but wasn't it always easy – too easy – to invent one?

"For you, Laszlo," she said. "Not for me. What would it be?"

"Well, for example," I began, not knowing where I was heading, but stumbling forward blindly, the clever graduate in English literature, "the good man dies and the rogue survives. So fate is random – is that the point? Or is it that the rogue's rebelliousness is really more deserving than the good man's obedience?"

I stopped, and then continued, warming to the sound of my own voice. "It might mean either or both those things – or something quite different. It's like something electric, or radioactive. It radiates meanings. It vibrates with possibilities. To come down hard and fast in favour of just one closes the door on all the others."

I looked at her eager, naïve, shrewd face. No, I hadn't lost her. She was with me. I said, "It's a piece of *theatre*, Heather. It's *there!*"

She was in that sitting-on-her-legs position on my bed, staring at me intently, her eyes shining as they always did when I talked like this. "Come here," she said. I scrambled out of the chair and joined her on that bumpy unyielding surface where she began to unbutton my shirt, pulling it off the shoulder. "I'm a bear," she said, "and I eat shoulders."

From that moment it was all a blur of urgency and (on my part) incompetence. I needed lessons, and in the weeks that followed Heather gave them. I was a good learner and keen to practice every day. This was what I've since come to think of as the Eden period of a love affair, when it's all joy and pleasure and uncomplicated. Neither thinks he/she has any rightful claim, statutory or moral, on the other. Each gives freely and takes gratefully. The sun shines, the night sky is full of stars, leaves rustle, streams flow, birds sing. A small clear strong uncluttered affection, manageable and sparkling, is born – like a lamb in spring, a kitten in its basket, a calf in the fold. No hint of the horns, the claws, the matted fleece of tomorrow. Heather and I fucked and were friends. What a great world it would be, I allow myself to think, if we could all be loving friends as Heather and I were then, without demands, without complications. It is, I'm assured by Louise, almost exclusively a male fantasy. It's certainly not achievable in the real world, or not for long. We are, male and female, cut out by our genes for greater, and nobler, and baser things.

It may be I exaggerate when I say "every day", but certainly for a brief time Heather and I did a lot of practicing. Things seldom seem as strange while they are happening as they can appear when looked back on. Sometimes when I climbed into bed with her, or grabbed her in the middle of her tiny kitchen, pulled up her skirt and pushed her back to be skewered against the wall, she would stop me and say, "You haven't *told* me anything." She was my teacher, but only on the understanding that I was hers.

She learned a lot about Elizabethan and Jacobean drama; and when I couldn't think of anything new to tell her about my own work, I told her about Rajiv's. Rajiv was now well into his new subject – not just the poetry and plays of W. B. Yeats, but the influence Indian poets and thinkers had exerted on them. It was under Hindu influence, Rajiv now believed, that Yeats had finally abandoned his own rationality – based Western cultural tradition in favour of the intuition and mysticism of the East; and this in turn had led on to his writing of the strange occult book he called *A Vision*. It was *A Vision*, my friend was now arguing, and not Irish nationalism, that formed the key to Yeats's life and work. Rajiv, in other words, was already well on the way towards the ideas put forth in his *W. B. Yeats and the Deeps of the Indian Mind*, the book on which his subsequent reputation has been based, and which was to propel him ultimately into one of the most prestigious Chairs of English Literature in his homeland.

Heather had an extraordinary memory for detail. Each item of knowledge I offered her was received like a small treasure, valued for itself, carefully stored and instantly available. I never saw any sign that these scraps were going to come together and form a larger picture. She had the temperament of a collector. The more items she had the more she wanted. "Tell me something," she would say; and as I described, let's say, a scene from the Essex rebellion (it had been preceded by a performance of Shakespeare's *Richard II*), the great Earl standing on his London roof trying to keep his dignity while bargaining with the forces of the Queen massing at his gate, her eyes would shine, that crooked smile would break out, and she would thank me in the only way she knew – a way which seemed to her hardly adequate, and to me a gross overpayment for something that cost me nothing. It was that rare kind of trade where both sides know they are scoring a bargain.

There was even a strange sense in which I felt Heather was

too demanding. Always asking what new fact I had discovered since she saw me last, or what new idea I'd had, she came close to discovering my secret – that for much of the time I was not doing academic work at all. I was already writing, spasmodically and without confidence (hence the secrecy), what was to be my first (and unpublished) novel, a story about two young people not unlike myself and Sammy, which I even thought of calling *The Secret History of Modernism*, because that was her title and she was to be the central character. Each day I took to the Reading Room, or to the Senate House Library, two schools notebooks ("Collins Graphic, wide-lined, sixpence"), one in which I was drafting a chapter of my novel, the other containing notes for one or another section of my Shakespeare project. I numbered the pages, and at the end of each week totted up scores in my diary. A graph of relative progress through that year shows Shakespeare clearly ahead in the early months, running neck-and-neck with Laszlo Winter in the middle months, and by Christmas lagging seriously behind.

Poor Shakespeare! He still lacks the benefit of my insights.

NINE

Old Rose and Old Reds

A FEW YEARS BACK A NOVEL OF MINE — IT WAS THE ONE before the last, called *No Going Back* — was reviewed in a New Zealand literary journal by Mendel Hand, a young novelist just then making a name for himself. Every male writer beyond a certain age (and there may be a female equivalent) cringes from such a notice, having been there himself, in the role of the young reviewer, and known the power of the Oedipal itch to dispose of literary fathers. This one was as bad as you might expect, and worse than you might hope for, because it wasn't only negative, it was exceptionally clever.

Mendel Hand was a recent graduate of an English Department, and his review was an exercise in "deconstruction", a method by which the critic comes at the work, so to speak, from the rear, discovering things the author, in the blind compulsions of composition, has done which run counter to his conscious intentions. The line Hand took was that my novels were full of poetry — quotations from the masters — and of a craving for poetry, and that every fiction I wrote hated itself for not being a poem. Further, he argued that because of this love of the concision and sharpness of poetry, I was bored by the necessity of having to body forth scenes, and so shirked my duties as a fiction writer. The effect, as it invariably is in "deconstruction", was to make the author seem a bumbling creature, a failure by his own measure, and the critic effortlessly superior.

When reviews first appear authors – and I think this is true of every one I've known – at first overreact to the negatives. We hardly notice the good things that are said – they are almost taken for granted. But every negative is a stab that leaves us bleeding. Much later, going back to look again, we take a more reasonable and dispassionate view, but by then the damage is done. The wounds have healed but the scars remain.

My first response to Mendel Hand's review was a decision that I would fell him with a single blow when next we met. In fact we had never met, but I'd seen his photograph. His face showed a rare quality of good humour and open intelligence, but I was in no mood to give him credit for that. What I paid more attention to was that he looked to be of no more than medium height and build, and not aggressive. I, on the other hand, am quite tall, and not invariably disinclined to violence. The idea of a single blow that would hurt and humiliate while earning me, a first-time offender, a non-custodial sentence, was consoling.

Louise, my in-house French diplomat, responded to this plan with a cautious circumlocution, pointing out that since Mendel Hand lived in another town six hundred kilometres to the south, I could not immediately carry it out, and suggesting that meanwhile it might be helpful if I read his first novel (she had read it) which had only recently appeared. This I did, and I will say now only that the young Hand had not allowed himself to fail in the way the old hand had. No corners were cut, no stones left unturned. Every scene was played out to the max. It was fiction without poetry, with all the taste and the tedium of real life.

Time passed and though I twice visited Mendel Hand's home town on literary business, I failed to meet him. By now I had completed another novel which would soon appear in the bookshops, and all my concern had shifted to its welfare. When at last Louise decided the time was right and I should re-read the offending review, I was struck again by its cleverness, but much less wounded by it. "Why should not old men be mad?" Yeats asks; and why, by the same token, should not young men be destroyers? I could feel the strength waning from my purpose. The prospect of another literary scandal attached to my name —

— WRITER PUNCHES CRITIC —
— LASZLO WINTER CHARGED WITH ASSAULT —
— "THE LITTLE SHIT DESERVED IT," SAYS NOVELIST —

faded and died.

I am reminded of this because these recollections have taken me back to the visit I made with Sammy to meet her Australian hero — heroine, she would then have said — the novelist Christina Stead, who told us (and it's a suggestion I've seen repeated twice recently, once in a novel by Saul Bellow, and once in a biography of George Orwell) that there is nothing more restorative to the authorial psyche than to spend a few minutes each day thinking up a painful death for your unkindest reviewer.

But once again I jump ahead of my story.

I hadn't seen Sammy for some time, but I'd been writing about her in that first shot of mine at novel-writing, so she was there always at the back of my mind, and sometimes at the front of it. One evening she rang at the street door at a moment when, lacking a shilling and wanting to light the gas and boil the kettle, I was trying to pick the padlock on the container into which the coins fell. "Let me in, Laszlo," she said into the intercom. "I bring tidings of great joy."

"I hope you bring a hairclip," I said. "Or a shilling."

I beamed her up, opened my white-enamelled door, and stood watching her in the dim ticking light as she climbed the green-carpeted stairs.

"She's here, she's here," Sam panted, arriving at the landing. Her eyes were bright, her face animated.

"Who's here?" I asked, helping myself to a clip from her hair.

She beat me away as the light switched itself off. "Guess, moron. Who do you think?"

"Christina Stead," I suggested, meaning only that I didn't have the faintest idea.

"Yes!" She jumped at me, kissed me full on the mouth and punched me in the solar plexus, pushing me against the door so it opened and the light from inside fell on us. "*Yes!*"

As I staggered backward into the entrance to my bed-sit I saw across the landing that the door opposite was opening, closing – then opening again as Heather, head down, hurried towards the shared bathroom. Catching the movement behind her, Sam half turned to look. "It's your neighbour," she said. "Hullo Feather."

"Shush," I said, pulling her in with me and closing the door. But I had laughed, as I always did when Sam invented new names for my neighbours and friends.

The "tidings of great joy" Sammy brought had come from Marx MacLaren. Christina Stead and her husband (lawful or *de facto*) Bill Blake, were back in London after their years in Europe and America. They were living in Hampstead, desperately short of money, and she was asking for work as a reviewer.

"And you'll never guess," Sam said. "Bill Blake – he's a Jew."

She loved to find parallels, but I didn't think this one was especially apt. "Bill Blake's a Jew," I said. "And Freddy Goldstein's a Jew. So what does that make you? Christina Stead?"

Sam looked hard at me. She wasn't used (neither was I) to my taking a salty independent tone with her. "Popeye's been eating his spinach," she said. "Good boy." She took off her coat and hung it over a chair. "Now listen."

I listened. In the morning we were going to visit Christina Stead – "we" because Sam felt she couldn't do it on her own. She needed support. But she had to meet this woman – *had to*. Marx MacLaren had said she could take a pile of books from which the novelist could choose two or three for review. He knew of Sammy's enthusiasm for the author of *For Love Alone* and *The Man who Loved Children*. "You're a fan. And you speak the same" (he'd said it, she thought, with just a faint curling of the lip) ". . . *strain* of English."

"Well too bad if he can't resist a sneer," she said. "He's being kind really – to Christina, because she needs the reviews, and to me, because he knows how much I want to meet her."

I said (as she knew I would) that I would go with her; but I was puzzled too. Why would Sam, who was no shrinker, need support?

"I might see her as my mother," Sam explained. "I might

falter. She's a powerful woman. She might think of me as a brainless girl and be tempted to step on me. Women can be like that sometimes. With a man there, she'll behave herself."

Next morning she was at my door ahead of time. I let her in and she waited, reading the paper while I shaved. As we came out on the landing and I stopped to double-lock my door Heather burst out of hers, pulled it shut with a bang, and rushed past us and down the stairs. Again her head was tilted forward and her shoulders lifted, the body language saying that she didn't mean to cross our paths and that she had no interest in us. She was wearing a matching woollen coat and hat in the colour I learned as a child was called view rose, and which I've thought since must be bad French – *vieux rose* – a not very attractive, darker-than-pink pink that called attention to itself. The coat collar had a trim of false fur and the hat was a beret – and wasn't there (or are memory and Sammy's name for Heather playing me false here?) a feather stuck through it? Sam leaned on the stair rail and watched her go, all the way to the front door and out. "Penny for the Guy," she murmured as the front door banged shut. This time I didn't laugh.

We went down the stairs, slowly, saying nothing. At the bottom Sam stopped, turned, and looked hard at me. "Why is she rushing about like that?"

I said I didn't know, hadn't the faintest idea, rushing about like what, who was rushing about?

Sam went on staring – reading me. "Isn't she your resident – you know . . . What the knave of hearts stole?"

"I don't know what she is," I lied. "But she's very nice."

I didn't blink, but neither did Sam. "This won't do," she

said; and she went on ahead of me, out the door and down to the street where 576AHY, battleship grey, was waiting to take us to Hampstead.

Christina Stead's address when we reached it proved to be a dingy red-brick tenement with a bell at street level that didn't work and didn't need to because the lock on the street door didn't work either. We climbed to the third floor and knocked. After a moment the door opened and Christina Stead looked out. She was tall, with a big bosom, good calves and ankles, thick tight hair and an expression that was casual, almost lazy. The top teeth, which had been prominent in a photograph Sam had shown me, didn't appear to be now; so they must be dentures, I decided, or the face must have changed, filled out.

Sam was making her explanations. Mr MacLaren had sent her with the books for review.

"What have you brought me?" the writer asked, smiling, opening the door a little wider but not inviting us in.

"I was hoping we might talk to you," Sam said. "Just for a few minutes. I'm from Sydney and I'm a great admirer of your work."

Christina Stead looked at her, not cold, not warm, just taking her in. "We're at work in here," she said.

Sam nodded. "I understand. I wouldn't want to interrupt." But the bag containing the books stayed on her shoulder.

So there was an impasse, momentary, as if these two were at loggerheads. Then Christina Stead laughed. It was a good-humoured laugh; even admiring. "All right," she said. "This flat's no place to entertain visitors, but come in."

We stepped straight into a small dark sitting room where a small dark man with his back to us was hunting for something among crowded bookshelves. On the table books and papers were spread out. But she led us straight on. "That's Bill," she said, without stopping. And more or less over her shoulder, "Bill, these two are from Marx MacLaren."

"Hullo," Bill Blake said, half-turning for politeness, but not really looking at us over the tops of his glasses. "Welcome to the Wailing Wall." And he bobbed his head a few times at the books.

In the kitchen her own typewriter was set up on the table. "I don't need to consult books," she said. "My work comes straight out of a frivolous head and a rapacious memory. Tea?"

She put the kettle on, nodding us towards chairs. "Now let me see these books."

We sat while she read the jacket copy, the opening para-graphs, some paragraphs in the middle. She took her time. The kettle whistled on the gas, she made tea in a too-large white enamel pot with black chips in its sides, and returned to the books, leaving it to brew. There was a strange calm about her, not of contentment but of something like resignation. "Things are as they are," it seemed to say, "and there's no use grumbling."

"I'll have these," she said, putting three books down on the table and patting their heads. She said she'd wasted a lot of time and energy cursing reviewers, and always felt guilty taking on the job herself. "But I need the dough," she said, putting on a Brooklyn accent. It was then she told us how restorative it was for the authorial psyche to commit the occasional mental murder on unfriendly reviewers.

"Does Mr MacLaren have a deadline?" she asked, pouring the tea. "I like to be strict about time."

I took this as a hint, a signal. She meant to give us our tea and have us out of there; and that, pretty much, was achieved, but there was time for Sam to pay tribute, say which books of Christina Stead's she especially admired and why.

Politics, Sam had been told by her boss, should be avoided. These two, Christina and Bill, were communists − Party members − and this was a bad time for the CP. In the previous year had come Nikita Khrushchev's address to the Twentieth Congress in which he'd said the unsayable − that the late Great Leader Stalin, the man idealists of the Left all around the world had thought of as History's Gift, had been a tyrant and a murderer. It had caused a wave of defections from Western communist parties. Those who hung on must have been thinking, "Well, it's a dreadful shock, but if the new man's able to denounce these evils, clearly now they must be a thing of the past."

But late in the same year had come the uprising against the Soviet-backed government of Hungary. The new "liberal" Mr Khrushchev, with his associate Bulganin, (Mr B and Mr K the British press were calling them) ordered in the Soviet tanks, and there were more defections.

So we avoided politics, and then it raised its head (as the avoided topic so often contrives to do) by accident. Christina Stead asked about my first name, Laszlo. I explained it came from my mother's Hungarian father, and there it was in front of us, unavoidable, my grandfather's homeland, the wishes of his people crushed by the tanks of the Red Army.

The silence was so awkward and so palpable something had to be said to fill it. "What's been happening there," the Party member said in a stiff, Party member tone, "has been ... unfortunate."

It might have come from a commissar and for Sammy it

wasn't enough. She wanted some kind of acknowledgement that a wrong had been done. "They say," she said, "that the Prime Minister . . . What's his name, Laszlo?"

"Imre Nagy," Christina Stead supplied, with the questioning inflexion of a school mistress who doesn't wish to have her time wasted.

"That he was strangled in a cellar."

"Yes they do say that." That was the Party member again, cool and dry. "Horrible," Sammy said. "The thought of it makes me . . ." She was suddenly vehement. "It makes me *sick*."

Christina Stead got up and went to the sink, not for anything in particular it seemed, because she stood there staring at nothing, the fingers of her two hands resting lightly on the edge of the bench. "Mistakes are made," she said. Her voice was tired as if her courage was gone.

Back in the street Sammy and I sat silent in the Ford Popular. After a few minutes she turned on the engine and we drove away. But we didn't get far before she pulled over and parked again. "D'you feel like coffee?"

We were seated with our hot drinks before she said anything about the visit, and then it was oblique — just a repetition of Christina Stead's "Mistakes are made," and a bitter shake of the head.

I said, "I thought there was something heroic about her. About both of them."

Sam scowled at me. "If we'd stayed she might have told us you can't make an omelette without breaking eggs."

"It's called solidarity, Sam."

"It's called stupidity, Laszlo."

"Look how they're living. And still battling on."

She shrugged, her face showing a relenting tendency. "Well

anyway, she can write, and that's what matters."

Sammy pointed down the street to a line of trees. "That's Highgate Cemetery, did you know? Karl Marx is buried there."

"And Coleridge," I said; and I quoted – chanted at her – the last section of "Kubla Khan", the lines about the damsel with a dulcimer, and the poet with his flashing eyes and floating hair who has fed on honeydew and drunk the milk of Paradise. She put her hand over mine and we sat looking, not at one another, but at the big trees screening the cemetery. "Marx and Coleridge, she said. 'That's a cruel conjunction isn't it?"

I wasn't sure what she meant, but I felt it was right, and that it had something to do with Christina Stead, committed both to literature and to politics and unable to disentangle them.

Back in Phillimore Gardens she thanked me for moral support. "And Saturday," she reminded. "Keep it free." There was to be a gathering of the gang – "the usual suspects" – at Castlenau Mansions. Rajiv would be there. And Margot, down from Oxford.

"Don't forget," Sammy said. "I'll collect you."

I mention that Saturday gathering because I see it now as an example of the way Sam kept a hand on the steering wheel of my life. She thought – though she didn't say – that Margot Derry would be good for me (better than "Feather"), and she contrived a way to bring us together. But at first things didn't go according to plan.

Among the young New Zealanders who knew one another in London and met at parties, or ran into one another checking for mail at New Zealand House in the Strand, there was a young writer, Dick Flinders. Dick had a moustache, a pipe and darkly horn-rimmed glasses. They were his props, and I was inclined to think he didn't have much else. But he did have confidence – or should I call it courage? Even before he'd published a word he always described himself as "a writer".

Then came his first book, a collection of short stories called *The South Sea Islanders*. On the back of the jacket there was a photograph of Dick on the Embankment, the stem of his pipe clamped in his teeth and the bowl grasped in his right hand. I handed the book around (it was now the Saturday afternoon and we were together in the big Castlenau Mansions kitchen) pointing out how strange it looked, as if the pipe was the handle by which Dick held his head on his shoulders.

Margot Derry at once took me to task for the tone – "sneering, sardonic, superior" – she said I always adopted when talking of Dick.

"*Always*," I repeated, and wanted to know when she'd heard me speak of him before.

But it didn't do to try to be smarter than Margot. "You mean you don't *always*," she said. "What do you say when you're not sneering, Laszlo?"

I told her that mostly I didn't say anything at all about him. It just happened that at this moment he'd published a book.

"And you're jealous," she said.

I thought of denying this, but then thought of something better. "If I'm jealous," I said, "it's not of the book. It's of the fact that he's been published."

She looked at me, taking this in. Margot liked fine distinctions. "So you're saying it's a bad book."

No I wasn't saying it even if I thought it. I said, "Margot, I thought you were safely in Oxford. If I'd known you were going to be here I wouldn't have mentioned Dick Flinders."

That's how it was between us: testy. It wasn't because we weren't interested in one another; it was because we were. Sam must have seen that in the short run we were heading for trouble – arguments, even unpleasantness – if she didn't intervene. But she was ready for that.

She contrived to corner the two of us together. She had, she explained, two tickets for tonight's performance of a play at the Lyric Hammersmith – *Danton's Death*. She'd been going to go with Freddy Goldstein but now it wasn't possible. They would go to it later. She was offering us the tickets. We could go together.

It was an offer we couldn't – neither of us – refuse. It forced us to be civilized to one another. And then the play itself, with Patrick McGoohan doing a cold steel Robespierre, was so exciting we came away bonded by the world he'd created and which we'd shared. We ate a pasta together, had a "last drinks" drink at a pub overlooking the river, took a late night stroll along the tow path.

By the time I delivered Margot back to the door of Castlenau Mansions where she was to spend the night, we were arm in arm, and closer than that – more like hand in glove. We kissed – affectionately. Margot said, "Next time you need to look for something in the Bodleian, why don't you make it a visit?" She rephrased it: "Come and visit me."

I said I'd love to. But I wasn't sure where . . . I would have to look into places . . .

"To stay? We'll sort that out," she said. "I'll talk to Mark and then I'll write." Mark was her brother, also at Oxford, reading history and making a name for himself as an athlete — a high jumper.

I walked home that night, all the way to Phillimore Gardens.

TEN

The Goldstein Story – 2

FRIEDRICH GOLDSTEIN HAD BEEN OLD ENOUGH TO BE aware that his father was banished from the house among pines on the slopes of Mount Carmel because he had done something wrong. This made the boy anxious, and the anxiety increased when Hilde took him back to Germany. Already he understood he was a Jew, or partly a Jew, and that in Germany it was not a good or a safe thing to be. Soon he was to hear his mother's family talking, in half whispers, sentences cut short when it was noticed he was listening, of "protecting little Freddy", even of "saving" him.

One memory he retained was of arriving on the platform of a railway station where Hilde was asked for their papers and, after a brief and frosty exchange, was told to follow the uniformed questioner into an office. Freddy was left beside a pile of luggage and told to wait. Time passed – it seemed to him a very long time – and he found himself on a platform now empty, feeling a kind of certainty-in-terror that he would never see his mother again, and that soon he would be taken away and something unspeakable would be done to him.

When Hilde came out of the office she was ruffled, insulted, angry. It was a mood which continued and increased during that year. Hilde's family didn't like the Nazis, but made excuses for them and praised their achievements. Germany's humiliation after the Great War, the Great Inflation, the Great Depression – how much more, they asked, could be loaded on a nation and a people, before the time came for them to assert their pride and reclaim what was rightfully theirs?

And yes, Hilde would concede, there was some truth in that. But if that was all there was at stake – a reassertion of national honour and pride – why were they, her own good Aryan family, always warning her not to raise her voice in public places, to be careful what she said on the telephone, and not to make jokes about Hitler and his cronies?

Hitler said he was not a dictator, he had only made democracy simpler. But what kind of democracy was it when you couldn't speak your thoughts, when books were burned, phones tapped, informers encouraged, and listening to foreign radio broadcasts forbidden on pain of imprisonment or death?

"You are all afraid," Hilde told them. "I can feel it. Fear. All Germany smells of it. How is that better than what we had before?"

And always, everywhere, there was the hate chorus against the Jews. Slogans: "The Jews are our Misfortune." "Whoever knows the Jew knows the Devil." "Synagogues are Dens of Thieves." "Who buys from Jews is a Traitor to the Nation."

In the newspaper she read of a "scientific study of the Jewish character" which showed it to be composed of "cruelty, hatred, violence, cunning and avarice". In a broadcast speech she heard Dr Goebells say that the Jews "should be exterminated like fleas and bedbugs".

"What has my Paul done to deserve this?" Hilde asked her family, overlooking for a moment his Latvian flower-seller, and perhaps already forgiving him his trespass. "He fought in the war. His brother fought and almost lost the use of his right hand. They are loyal Germans. What have they done to deserve being described as vermin?"

Her father always agreed with her. The Goldsteins had done nothing. He had a formula that went, "For individual Jews like Paul and his family I can only say . . ." His expressions of sympathy always came first. He would concede (lowering his voice) that the Nazis "laid it on too strong". But then he would begin to echo – tentatively, not wanting to set his daughter off into what he called her "sentimental rages" – the Party propaganda. How was it that, before Hitler began to sort things out, *so many* of Germany's lawyers and bankers and businessmen had been Jews? How was it they had remained rich while Germany went through its years of defeat and poverty and humiliation? Hadn't they been pulling the strings to suit themselves? Of course they had!

Hilde wanted to visit the Goldsteins. They were Freddy's grandparents. They would want to see him again. Her father warned against it. The Jews, he said, now more than ever had their own separate network of friends, family, schools, welfare organisations. Fraternising with them was discouraged. It would do them no good, and it might be held against her.

"I'm the wife of a Jew," she pointed out. "The mother of a *Mischling*."

"But you're suing for divorce," her mother reminded her.

"No I'm not," she told them. "I've withdrawn my application." This was not true. She had only at that moment thought of it, but she meant it. In the midst of an argument with her family, whom she had come to think of as Germany itself, she had arrived at a decision. Hilde had never until that moment thought of herself as having a role in something that might be called History. Now she did feel it, and it seemed there was only one right thing for her to do. A loyalty was required of her, and she would give it. It simplified her life. It made Paul's infidelity and her jealousy insignificant, trivial, irrelevant. It made it easier for her to decide, and to act.

She found the Goldsteins in a state of alarm, anxiety and distress. Their jewellery business was finished. Aryan customers, many of whom perhaps pitied them but feared being called "Traitors to the Nation", had gone elsewhere. Others, who saw this as a way of giving practical expression to their National Socialist ideals, refused to settle accounts. Jewish customers remained loyal, but few were in a position to buy what the Goldsteins lived by selling.

Special "Jew taxes", and petty regulations maliciously enforced, had brought the business close to bankruptcy. Joachim had put it up for sale and then withdrawn it when he learned what meagre prices were offered and how much of this would have to be given up in "Reich Flight Tax" if they decided to emigrate. Later he changed his mind but it was too late. He was told that if he planned to leave, anything that remained of the business would be appropriated.

Finally on the night of 9 November, 1938, which came to be known as *Kristallnacht*, when thousands of Jewish small businesses throughout Germany and Austria were smashed or burned by rampaging Nazis, all that remained of the shop was plundered and destroyed. A month later, as if to mark this great victory over Jewish commerce, a Day of German Solidarity was celebrated from noon until 8 p.m., during which time Jews were confined by a curfew to their homes.

The elderly couple were living now on a small secret hoard

of cash and jewellery. It was all they had; but if it should be discovered it could mean the concentration camp. A decree required that Jewish assets should be declared. Nothing was to be hidden from the Reich, since anything owned by a Jew could be considered stolen from the German people. They had at last put their names down on lists of applicants for visas to escape to some place of safety, but the lists were long, the exodus was meeting resistance at every point, and they must have known they had left it too late.

Klaus and his family, it seemed, were going to be more fortunate. In a letter Paul had urged his brother to get out while there was still time. "Take the parents if you can. If they won't go, or can't, then at least save your children."

Klaus hesitated, still saying over to himself like a mantra that his war wound and his Iron Cross would protect them. The force of the mantra waned until he no longer believed it. Fear – the growing sense of menace all around them – forced him to accept that they must go. It took time and patience, persistence and bribes, but at last he got their names down for Cuba, said to be the best chance of a quick escape and subsequent entry to the United States. They were booked on a liner, the *St Louis*, that would leave Hamburg for Havana on 13 May, 1939.

Meanwhile the humiliations continued and got worse. Joachim, who for a time after the business was ruined had tried to beat the terrible apathy that crept over him by reading every day in the public library, had been told that as a Jew he could no longer use the reading rooms. Borrowing rights were also denied. For a part of one summer he and Beatrice took to driving into the countryside, taking a picnic in a hamper, forgetting politics in the contemplation of nature. That had lasted only a few months until it was decided all Jews' driving licences were cancelled.

Movies had been another escape; but late in 1938 the Berlin Chief of Police ordered that Jews were forbidden to enter certain listed public places. Cinemas were included. Other places denied them were concert-and lecture-halls. There were a few modest restaurants where they could still eat, but more and more of these put up the sign "Jews not welcome", until there was only the railway station left.

Everywhere the Goldsteins looked or listened there was malice directed at them. An exhibition toured the country, "The Eternal Jew", featuring "hook-nosed intellectualism" and its threat to the well-being of the Reich. Its theme was "Blood determines Character and Soul. Once the Jew has spoiled your Blood and Soul you are dead for Race and Fatherland."

Synagogues were burned. Rabbis were chased in the street, beaten, their beards set alight. New Jewish identity cards were issued, with a large J and the owner's fingerprints. Jews with "Aryan" names had to add a Jewish forename – usually Israel for a male, Sara for a female. The message, and the contradiction, were now always the same – the Goldsteins were not wanted, but nor could they easily leave. Joachim and his wife talked about suicide, and how it might be done. At night they went to bed thinking, "Will they come for us tonight?" and wondering how they would die – gunshot? Blows to the head? Stab wounds? Burned to death in their own home? They hoped if it happened they would be allowed to die together. Even in their worst imaginings, even in their nightmares, the possibility that they might die in a gas chamber never figured.

It had taken Hilde some time to find them. There was a phone number listed in the book but when she tried to call there was never an answer. The doors to their garden court-yard were securely locked, barricaded from the inside, and when she knocked, and rang the bell, there was no reply. At a second attempt she stood silent, listening, and was sure she heard voices within. She called to them, attracted their atten-tion, and succeeded in speaking to them through the gate.

They were overjoyed to see her, and lavished so much love and attention and cake on little Freddy he retained, decades later, more vivid memories of them than of Hilde's parents with whom he spent more time. Joachim explained about the phone. "They know our connections in the Jewish community. I'm sure it's tapped, so we've made a rule never to use it. When it rings we don't answer."

They talked of Paul. Beatrice wept and, together, the older couple begged Hilde to go back to him. They had heard from him, and from the Rabbi who had looked after him. He was full of remorse and promises of fidelity. He loved Hilde and missed her, and he missed Freddy and feared for what would become of him in Germany.

"What he has done to you is unforgivable," Beatrice said, "but you must forgive him, if only for the sake of the child. Little Freddy must be saved."

How the second departure from Germany was achieved Friedrich Goldstein didn't know – only that once again it had been easier for Hilde to travel because she was not Jewish. He remembered the sense of an impending crisis, endless talk about money, a race against time – and then sad farewells, first to one set of grandparents and then to the other, after which there was a train journey to Genoa, and the feeling that an escape had been effected. Once again he and his mother were at sea, and once again at the end of the voyage was the city of Haifa.

But meanwhile there had been more explosions in Palestine, clearer signs that the Arabs were going to resist the idea of a Jewish homeland. Paul, still anxious about their future, had been working to find a route to another and safer haven. Hilde had brought money from her own family that would pay fares to take them there.

The reunited trio spent five or six months in the house among the Mount Carmel pines before setting off again. After weeks at sea and several ports of call they sailed into Auckland. Jewish families long established there had set up committees to welcome and help refugees from Germany. Paul found employment – not at once as a doctor, that would come later – but first as a storeman packer, then as travelling salesman for a Jewish owned company.

It was summer and the school Freddy attended had a swimming pool. After seeing the other boys stripping off in the changing sheds he reported at home that all but two or three of the boys in his class were Jews. His parents were puzzled until Paul discovered that male circumcision in New Zealand had in recent years become very nearly universal. Vast distance had conspired with a strange fad of the medical profession to make New Zealand seem an ideal hiding place.

ELEVEN

The Wind in the Willows

MY LIFE DURING THOSE YEARS IN ENGLAND WAS FULL of attacks of embarrassment. Often there was good cause, but there didn't have to be. I could wake in the night and feel it acutely – not shame, not guilt, just embarrassment – and I would have to run through the events of the previous day until I found something, anything, to attach it to. It was a depressive tendency – like (but not so serious) being burdened with groundless guilt; and I came to see it also as a kind of egotism.

Self-absorption is slow death by interior corrosion, and what protects us against it is curiosity, an appetite for the world in all its forms. If you enjoy the world enough to look hard at it, it will save you – but only from yourself, not from disease, war, man-eating tigers or other people, all of which are part of what you must love (or at least love to look out at) in order to live well.

Even my successful evening at the theatre with Margot Derry left me wincing in the night, thinking I must have appeared foolish and that I wouldn't hear from her again. But a day or so later the promised letter came, inviting me to Oxford, suggesting when I should come and where I should stay. She was in rooms in St Anne's, but Mark, her brother, was in digs not far away. There was a spare bed, and his landlady, easy-going and fond of Mark, never objected if he had male friends to stay.

Margot suggested I come at once and stay a few days – even a week. Mark, she assured me, would be glad of the company of someone from New Zealand with whom he could "be himself". She and I could work together (she was doing a paper on Shakespeare's contemporary, Ben Jonson) and exchange ideas. She enclosed a timetable for the trains.

In the days before I left for Oxford I saw Heather only in passing. She continued to "rush about", waving to me, exchanging brief greetings on the stairs, but behaving as if there was never a moment in which to stop and talk. Was it particularly busy at "the shop"? I didn't think so, and the baritone lady never called.

So then, I decided, the problem must be jealousy. But how could someone who slept with three or four different men each week be jealous? I watched her. I observed those strange headlong, head-down dashes, and how they seemed both to keep me at bay and to ask to be noticed. I was sure that if I tried to talk about it she would say I was imagining things, that there was no problem. I wanted to answer what she seemed to be telling me but I didn't know how. Perhaps my own body language signalled replies – protesting innocence, indignation. If it did, was she capable of reading them? Were we in fact conducting a wordless dialogue up and down the stairs, or was it all one way? In the meantime I offered her no new enlightenment about Shakespeare and his theatres, and she looked for none. Our local skills-based economy had ceased trading.

I decided I must leave her a note to say I was going to

Oxford for a few days to study in the Bodleian. This would make it clear that my absence had nothing to do with Sammy. But then it occurred to me that to do anything which suggested I owed her an explanation might also be read as a declaration. In those days there was a semi-official scale of attachments, each one leading on to the next: girlfriend and boyfriend, engagement, marriage. If I had a responsibility to explain myself to her, what would that imply?

When Sammy had cruelly described Heather as our resident tart, I'd winced, and I winced again each time I thought of it. It wasn't that she'd been putting Heather in her place. She didn't care about Heather. She was putting me in mine, in case her hunch that something was going on between us might be right. She was applying a puff of weedkiller to the soil at 9 Phillimore Gardens, so that any little romantic shrub that might be germinating there would come up with withered leaves and a brown stem. In this I'm sure she thought she was doing me a favour. Perhaps she was.

Looking back I can distinguish three selves that went into talks about Heather. There was the young animal who could not think about her without remembering her body engaged with his in the act of sex. Second was the social pragmatist, who argued that however much the animal might enjoy the games he'd played with her, there was a whole world outside the bedroom in which there was no common ground on which they could meet. This brought the third self into play – the sensitive, affectionate person who disliked intensely the thought of causing pain.

By far the strongest of these three was the young animal. If the others were to be heard they had to offer an alternative. The hope of one lay in Margot Derry's letter. Without wanting to make simple and crystal clear what was in fact blurred and uncertain, still I think it's true, or true enough, to say I went to Oxford wanting to be rescued from Heather before I hurt her any further. It was a kind of male-to-female arrogance, I now see, which underestimated Heather's strengths and over-estimated my own; but it was innocent, well-intentioned.

Margot met me at the station, the complete Oxford under-graduate (her New Zealand degree was discounted) wearing a ragged gown over her twin-set and wheeling a battered bike. We put my haversack on the bike and walked together. She took me a roundabout route, between the river and the canal, under big trees, along the backs of houses, over bridges that crossed this way and that. There were barges moored on the canal, and people drinking beer and cooking meals on primus stoves. Smoke drifted across, and the fragrance of singeing sausages.

Then we turned right, into the town. At the Gardener's Arms, a tiny pub in a narrow lane, Mark was waiting – tall, good-looking, ruddy-cheeked and wet-haired, just back from the Iffley Road track where he had been training. There was quite a gathering of people, his friends and Margot's, who met there. I was introduced to some of them, and was to meet them at intervals during my stay.

Mark and Margot were an unusual pair. In temperament and convictions they were different, but they never quarrelled and were always fiercely defensive of one another. I learned very early that if I didn't want to displease Margot I should never say anything negative, or even "clever", about her brother. Conversely, a short-cut to her good books was to say something – anything at all – complimentary about him.

Margot called herself a socialist but it was explained in a way that made her sound more like a Sunday school teacher. Mark had no political convictions. I felt that temperamentally he was a Tory, though an unpredictable and rebellious one. He tended to boil and seethe at times, but never spoke out or committed himself publicly.

Margot had said Mark would like to spend time with a compatriot. He said so himself as he greeted me and we shook hands. But I noticed that he'd begun to sound more like a Pom than a New Zealander. Like his sister, he was somewhat patrician. By that I suppose I mean he had a code of behaviour to fall back on even at times when a dark cloud crossed his brow suggesting he might be inwardly tormented and confused. He was fitting easily (though with routine complaints and protests) into the ways of his College and the University. He wore the special ties, attended the dinners, had been elected to Vinsons. Socially adept, even adroit, he could be a hearty with the hearties and with the aesthetes an aesthete.

What mattered most to him was his high jumping. I went to the track sometimes and watch him working at it. In those days what's called the Fosbury Flop hadn't been invented, and couldn't have been. The athlete cleared the bar and fell, from whatever height he'd jumped, into a pit of raked sand. To fall six feet on to the back of the head and neck would have been lethal, and the new jump has only been made possible by the piles of foam which break the fall.

Mark's style was the Straddle. He paced out his run-up, stood staring long and hard at the bar imagining (as he explained to me) his body clearing it. Then at a certain moment he would find himself already into his run. There was no decision to begin, just repeated imagining of it, then a moment of blankness and the discovery of himself already a couple of paces into the seven of his approach.

That first evening they took me to a poetry reading at the Oxford Union. The poets were two American Beats, Allen Ginsberg and Gregory Corso, who weren't at that time famous (or not in England) and hadn't acquired the long hair and beads, the rope-and-leather look that would come a few years later. Flower power was still waiting in the wings; but Corso looked striking enough, "bohemian" we would have called it, in a big black leather coat and white trousers. Ginsberg looked like what he then was, a young intellectual Jew from Paterson, New Jersey, graduate of Columbia University, in horn-rim glasses, corduroy trousers, tweed jacket and tie.

Towards the end of the reading there were interruptions from the floor and an argument blew up because some of the undergraduates thought a poem of Corso's about the atomic bomb ("O bomb I love you", it went, "I want to kiss your clank") treated the subject as a joke. This had to be argued out, pro and con, and meanwhile the poets rolled their eyes at one another, exchanged bored glances and passed notes back and forth.

St Anne's, not one of the ancient and beautiful Colleges with cloisters, quads and gardens, was a cluster of very large, brown-brick Victorian houses looking out on Banbury Road. It was only a short walk from where Mark had his digs, and quite near to what was called the University Parks, an area of many acres, with cricket pitches and pavilions, playing fields, lawns, gravel paths and gardens.

This was bounded by the Cherwell, the smaller of the two

rivers that flow through Oxford. There was a footbridge that
made a high bow over the river, and once over it you were
out of the parks and into fields, water meadows and wood-
land. There were waist-high grasses, nettles and sometimes
reeds, with lines of willows and poplars, through which passed
beaten clay paths and deep drains. It was what I thought
of as Wind in the Willows territory, and Margot and I used
to puzzle over how it was that although almost everything
growing there (apart perhaps from the nettles) had been
imported into New Zealand, and in some farming areas
could be seen even to the exclusion of anything indigenous,
so there were scenes twelve thousand miles away which
reproduced this one almost tree for tree and flower for flower
and blade for blade, still there was some subtle but unmis-
takeable difference. Was it the light? Or a quality of the air?
Whatever it was, this was the original, the other a forgery. A
brilliant forgery, even perhaps an improvement, but not the
original.

Margot and I walked there each morning before going
to work at the Bodleian – sometimes along the river's edge,
sometimes on paths that took us into what was then a wilder-
ness of green.

At that time of year every hour was family hour on the
stretch of water either side of the footbridge. There was a
moorfowl family – cock, hen and five or six chicks; and two
or three sets of duck parents with ducklings. The young were
lively, growing fast, but as yet still downy. But the family
we kept a particular watch on was a pair of white swans
and their two grey-downed cygnets. Mother father son and
daughter, we decided; and we invented together a predictable
and boring English novel in which they figured as graceful

aristocrats of the river, charming and unaffected compared to the noisy pushy middle-class ducks and the scruffy squabbling working-class moorfowls. We had names for them all, only some of which I now remember.

One morning there was only one swan anywhere in sight of the bridge. We hunted up and down but the other parent bird and the two cygnets were gone. We crossed the bridge and at last found them in one of the willow-sheltered drains that ran through the fields. These were not usually navigable to the swans but there had been rain upriver and the Cherwell had risen and flowed back into them. The mother swan, absolutely still on the still water, her head looking down (and, reflected, looking up) from its white column of neck, watched over the cygnets while they made a meal of some kind of weed that grew there.

We stood side by side watching the mother watching her young. After a time Margot took my hand. "Come," she said. We waded through long grass, avoiding nettles as far as we could. Under a willow, far from the path and out of sight in the long grass, she spread her gown, I spread my jacket, and we lay down together.

I'd got used to Heather's love-making which was ebullient, full of talk and bounce, jokes and action. With Margot it was quieter, more inward and silent, as if she was tasting something subtle and delicious that needed concentration so it could afterwards be precisely described. She kept her eyes closed; and at the moment of intensity when she opened them, lifting her head slightly, she seemed to stare past me over my shoulder, so on that first occasion I looked around thinking someone must be there, looking down at us. After that moment she was always languid, good humoured, accommodating. I could do what I liked with her body. It was mine.

She liked me to quote poetry in her ear – seventeenth century love poetry, especially of the tough and urgent rather than the sweetly lyrical kind; and since I had a head full of it, I could usually oblige. There was even a joke between us that the M-poets were best – Marvell for example:

> *Now* therefore while the youthful hue
> Sits on thy skin like morning dew
> And while thy willing soul transpires
> At every pore with instant fires
> *Now* let us sport us while we may
> And *now* like am'rous birds of prey . . .

– where each *now* could be an urgent thrust. Or it might be Marlowe:

> Treason was in her thought
> And cunningly to yield herself she sought
> Wherein Leander on her quivering breast
> Breathless spoke something, and sigh'd out the rest.

Even Milton, carefully culled, could do a quiet turn:

> These lull'd by nightingales embracing slept
> And on their naked limbs the flowery roof
> Shower'd roses . . .

It was strange, but during the short time that we were lovers I knew that I wasn't in love with Margot and would never be, partly (but only partly) because she was not and would never be in love with me. We were fond of one another. She was affectionate, kind, even grateful; she was also remote and mysterious.

Several things about her puzzled me. One was that nothing in her conversation ever suggested that she'd had lovers, or even one lover. She talked about her life in a tone that seemed frank enough. Now and then when a student friend was mentioned I asked, "A boyfriend?" Each time the answer was something like, "I suppose yes, in a way. It wasn't serious."

If I then asked "Were you lovers?" or "Did you sleep with him?" there was always an instant laugh and an entirely convincing, "No of course not."

So were there no other lovers? I couldn't believe there hadn't been at least one. Nothing seemed to be happening for the first time. She knew what she wanted from me, and how to get it. But when I did once push the question – was I her first lover? – she looked uncertain, whether about the fact, or how to answer, I couldn't tell, and then asked me why it mattered. We should be looking forward, she said, not back.

After that she contrived not only to change the subject but to make me feel it would be wrong, insensitive, to ask the question ever again.

When I returned to London from that first stay in Oxford there was no sign of Heather. I listened out for her, looked for her. There was no light under her door. One evening I saw Harry Pulsford letting himself into her room. He saw me watching from my door and came across the landing to explain. Heather's mother in Bristol was ill and needed looking after. She'd asked him to water her pot-plants and feed her goldfish while she was away.

Sammy phoned. She didn't ask about Margot but I knew she was listening to everything I said, keen to pick up the slightest hint or tremor that would tell her what was going on. I gave nothing away. I didn't know why, but I was angry with her.

But now she made another of those ticket offers I couldn't refuse. Freddy had cleared a night when he would be free to go to something with her – theatre or music, he left it to her to make the choice. Wagner's Ring Cycle was being done at Covent Garden and she'd bought two tickets for *Die Walkure*. Freddy was shocked and refused to go. He said Wagner was an anti-Semite whose music had been favoured by the Nazis. He'd been Hitler's favourite composer.

Sam had known nothing of this and was hurt when he told her such ignorance was shameful. She knew only that Wagner was a name attached to what were said to be great operas. She was angry with Freddy. "Are his operas about Jews?" she wanted to know. He said he didn't know what they were about and he didn't care. Actually he thought they were about gods and heroes and giants and dwarfs but that was hardly the point. This was music that had been played at Hitler rallies. It was tainted for ever. He couldn't imagine that any Jew who had lost family in the Holocaust would ever listen to it. Would she ask him to go to a poetry reading if Hitler was one of the poets?

She said she might if he was a good poet, and hung up.

Like Sam, coming from what then seemed the end of the earth, I hadn't heard a Wagner opera either and knew him only as one of the names that signified musical "greatness". Since arriving in London she and I had been voracious and shameless consumers of culture, soaking up as much music, theatre and art as we could find and could afford. She knew I would come with her.

If you discover yourself to be a Wagner person, the first time you hear one of his operas is an experience never forgotten. I don't know what Sam made of it. Afterwards we didn't talk; or if we did, I don't remember what was said. I knew next to nothing of the Ring Cycle. *Die Walkure* was sung in German and there were no surtitles, so I knew only what I could gulp down from the programme notes. But I was swept away by it, by the music, by the drama, by the music-drama; by the depth and range of its passion. Above all I was deeply affected by the love duets of the brother and sister, Siegmund and Sieglinde, whose incestuous love is to produce the hero, Siegfried.

Is it obvious where this is heading? At some point during that opera an image entered my consciousness – like the shadow of something. It was of Mark Derry's face at the moment before he began his run-up to the high jump bar. That face became Margot's at the moment of orgasm, which became Mark's again. The image was very beautiful, because the love of the brother and sister, Siegmund and Sieglinde, was beautiful. It had come to me like a moment of perfect insight, as if an archangel had tapped me on the shoulder and whispered (not wanting to disturb the music) "Excuse me, Sir. Message from God." The message was that these two, Mark and Margot, were, or had been, lovers. In my imagination it all fell into place like a story. They still loved one another but had decided their incest, if it wasn't wrong, was certainly dangerous, an addiction that might destroy them socially and had to be broken; or had to find some means to hide itself. I had been chosen as Margot's substitute lover. Mark knew this, accepted it, was party to it, and was made unhappy by it. This explained the agonised look that passed over his face from time to time. He didn't hate me, but he hated the necessity which I represented.

Later, as this conviction took root, and as I was removed from the music of Wagner which gave it beauty and nobility, it took a darker tone. I began to think of the three of us as characters in a novel by Henry James – *The Golden Bowl*. Supposing I had continued with Margot and we had married – would Mark always have been somewhere nearby? Was I to be Maggie Verver to their Charlotte and the Prince? These two, brother and sister, were not just too clever for me; they had been darkly, sinisterly, clever. I imagined them talking about me, planning, co-ordinating their stories, manipulating. I thought I could remember moments in the Gardener's Arms when I'd seen them exchanging secret smiles in the pub mirror.

At this point in my narrative I need to add quickly, before you dismiss me as insane, that while I entertained this idea I was not – or not consistently and completely – convinced of its truth. Some part of me believed it; some other part remained sceptical. But it affected my view of what had happened in Oxford and I wasn't able to respond easily and naturally to Margot's notes and phone calls. I was cordial, but the cordiality was forced. It can't have been long before she recognized that what had begun between us was already over.

A week, a fortnight went by and then she turned up one evening in London, at Phillimore Gardens. She brought good coffee, a cake with lemon icing, some dried fruit, chocolate, and almonds. I tried to be welcoming but I was nervous, uncertain. She took control, put me at ease, insisted I go on with my work while she prepared the small feast.

When it was ready we sat together at my little square table on which she had spread a lacy cloth that came with the bed-sit and which I seldom used. We drank the coffee and ate the good things. At last she said, "Tell me what's happened, Laszlo? What went wrong?"

I hadn't prepared an answer to this question though I must have known it would be asked, and so it was a surprise to myself that an answer not only came instantly, but came with total conviction. "I'm in love," I told her. And then, "With Sammy."

"But you were always in love with Sammy."

"Was I?"

"Of course. Didn't you know?"

I shook my head and said no, I didn't think I had known.

"But you know now."

"Yes."

"Are you lovers?"

"No, of course not. There's Freddy Goldstein."

"Oh . . ." She shrugged, impatient. "You'll have to do something about that."

She moved out of her chair and went to kiss me. I must for a moment have shrunk away. She laughed and told me to relax. "I'm not going to make you do that to me any more, I promise. But we're friends aren't we?"

Make me? It was as if my will in what had happened had been taken away from me, like a confiscated passport. "Yes of course," I said. And then, wanting to make some kind of apology I stumbled into a series of "It isn't that I . . . It wasn't that I . . ." statements, none of them completed.

"I understand," she said; and I felt that, probably, she did.

I let her kiss me now. It was a kind of goodbye kiss, full of irony, like a pat on the head.

In the days that followed I felt flat, purposeless. I felt I'd been in love with Sammy all along and hadn't known it until saying it to Margot; but now I did know and it made me unhappy. There was also some part of me that clung to the image of that place beside the Cherwell, the avian life on the water, our white bodies under blue sky and green willow pendants – wishing something more could have come of it, and wondering whether it had been enhanced or destroyed by a habit of mind and imagination which had to turn everything into a story.

Years later – ten years to be exact – I was once again, briefly, in Oxford. I'd spent the intervening decade in New Zealand, making my difficult way as a writer, keeping myself afloat with literary columns, long-distance script-doctoring, reviews for Sydney and Melbourne papers, contract work in the South Pacific for *National Geographic* and the *Readers' Digest*, while all the time working at the fiction which was what I really wanted to do. My first novel had had respectful reviews and unimpressive sales; my second, for which there were both British and American publishers, was just being launched, and I was back in the Northern Hemisphere on a modestly funded promotional tour organised by a new agent. It was no big deal, but for me as writer it was a move forward.

This was right at the end of the 1960s – a time of continuing Cold War threat and counter-threat, and of social turbulence in the West. The Vietnam War, and the protest against America's part in it, were raging. So was the social and sexual revolution that went with it. I was no longer "young" but, not yet into my forties, young enough to be affected. During the Suez crisis Anthony Eden had said it was as if the Canal ran through the sitting room at Number Ten. Now the Mekong was flowing through all the bedrooms of the West.

My first marriage was in the process of breaking up, breaking down, falling over, crashing – all my fault, of course, but that is another story and needs, here, only a sentence or two. Evrodiki and I had been living apart for most of a year. Now she wanted to go and live in Sydney where she had a sister and other friends and relations with whom she could speak her own language. She would take our two children. She was lonely and unhappy and I knew it would be wrong – and self-defeating – to put obstacles in her way.

So although I'd looked forward to this return to my old haunts, this was not a happy time for me, and cheap hotels are not good places to be unhappy in.

It was only an overnight visit I made to Oxford, with a book signing at Blackwells. There had been a notice about it put up somewhere in the shop but nobody came. I signed a small pile of books for future buyers and was free to amuse myself. I walked about the town, visited the University Parks and the fields beyond where I'd had my Wind in the Willows romance with Margot, finding them almost unchanged. That evening I found the Gardener's Arms where I'd drunk with Mark and his friends. I wondered whether I might find the same crowd. I didn't – not the crowd – but there was one I recognized, a New Zealand-born don who lived nearby and with whom I'd had a brief and rather peppery exchange about our homeland.

He was drinking with a lively group of friends but I found a moment to catch his attention. I told him we'd met briefly ten years before, and asked whether he knew what had become of Mark and Margot.

"Ah the Derrys," he said. "Gone, I'm afraid. Some years ago. To Canada, I believe."

"Both of them?" I asked.

"Yes yes. Both." It was said in a tone that implied, "Of course. What else?" And then I thought he hesitated, as if he was seeing the point of my question. Why would they go together? He'd thought of them – I was sure of it – as husband and wife, and then recalled that they were brother and sister.

"Sorry I can't tell you more," he said.

I thanked him and took my drink away to a quiet corner by an open window that looked out on a garden. Once again I had my story, and once again I didn't quite believe it, except in the way one believes a fiction and is able to insist on its truthfulness.

TWELVE

Only Connect

COMING FROM THE LAVENDER SURROUNDS OF OTTO
Stilz's pool just now I lowered my dripping self down on
warm stone steps between the pink and the dark red flower-
ing oleanders and in doing so maimed a large black ant
which managed, none the less, to deliver to my thigh a sting-
ing retaliatory nip. In the scale of Nature, however, which
expresses itself in an instant and with no need of thought, a
small bite to a human is much more serious than major
injury to an ant, and the latter was awarded a *coup de grace*,
after which I assuaged a twinge of guilt with the thought that
if I had been one of the Master Race who occupied France
in the years of my childhood, nine fellow ants would also
have gone to their deaths as additional reprisal.

Now I must explain myself.

After our visit to Otto Stiltz's Auckland apartment, which
broke my writer's block, our summer ran on and ran out,
followed by whatever it is one calls what comes next – a
"sort of" autumn in which such European trees as there are
do their best to be colourful (much as we human transplants
do our best in December to be "Christmassy"), followed by
a "sort of" winter in which there is no snow, only two or
three frosts, and quite enough rain thank you. These are not

so much my own reflections (I enjoy our seasons, and to me they are sufficiently differentiated) as Louise's.

Long ago I wrote a novel in which a New Zealander on a protracted visit to Europe married a Frenchwoman who returned with him to settle in Auckland. Having been encouraged by certain myths enshrined in her childhood reading to romanticise our general region (which she called "ze Souse Seas"), she suffered a disillusion that might have been forestalled if, before ever leaving *la belle France*, she had made a thoughtful study of the moods and subjects of her compatriot Gaugin's paintings of the Pacific. Many years later, life imitating art – or (a cynic might suggest) the fiction writer failing to attend to the truths of his own imagination – I married just such a Frenchwoman who has suffered just such a disillusion. Auckland, Louise considers, does not have a summer, and certainly has no winter; and how, she asks, can what divides these *soi-disant* seasons be properly called autumn and spring? It is all "one big mixed salad", she considers, with too much of everything (black cloud and blue sky, storm and calm, damp and dry) one after the other and often all at once, and with a big bad sun that breaks from cover now and then shooting from the hip before you have time to run indoors for your *'at*. Too much *wezzer* we *'ave*, according to Louise, and not enough *sezzons*. Her sense of what is *propre* is offended by such disorder, such unpredictability.

I tell her the old joke: If you don't like Auckland's weather, just wait an hour. She is not amused, especially because I deliver it in my Peter Sellers / Captain Clouseau accent and voice.

Once she complained, "Why did not you warn me?"

"I believe I did," I replied (thinking more about the

interesting word-order than the question). "And in any case, if you had read my books . . ."

"Oh your books," she said, with a rude French shrug. "*Pouf!*"

Well "*Pouf!*" or not, darling, they are my life, my *raison d'être*; and that is part of the trouble. As soon as the writer's block was removed which had caused me to think of giving up my trade altogether, I threw myself into the new work, and have been at it ever since – moving forward slowly, as is my habit, but writing every day, and with a concentration, a narrowness of focus that my old friend Rajiv might say (borrowing from his hero Yeats) is "like the watch mender, his magnifying glass caught in his screwed-up eye". In other words, I have been neglecting Louise.

Meanwhile Otto Stiltz, having returned to his adopted home in France, wrote, not just once briefly but at intervals and at length, urging us to come and share with him something of the French summer and the French way of life in the region made famous by names like Tartarin of Tarascon, songs like "*Sur le Pont d'Avignon*", stories about Alphonse Daudet's mill and M. Séguin's goat, and paintings like Van Gogh's *Café at Night at Arles*. So, to make the business a great deal simpler and briefer than it was (doesn't Virginia Woolf say the hardest job of the novelist is to get her characters from one room to the next? – and changing countries these days is much like moving to the next room), Louise was eager, I was willing, and we went!

My work was portable. I knew I could write it anywhere, and that is what I have been doing. I also knew there were parts of it, especially those concerning Samantha Conlan, that Otto Stiltz could help me with.

So we have been enjoying the wine and the food, the wine and the weather, the wine and the wine – a partial cure for an excess of which is the breath-taking chill, when the air temperature is up close to or beyond 30° C, of swimming a few miles downstream from the Pont du Gard, that remarkable Roman triple aquaduct (one built on top of another to carry a third) which Otto long ago signalled in my address book as the "P. du G.".

Now for a few days I am alone, in charge of Otto's house and his garden and his cat, he having gone to sort out some family business in Tübingen and then to watch the final of the European Cup (he is a football fanatic), Louise to visit her mother and to check on the progress of Jean-Claude, her son by her first marriage, who lives at present with his grandmother in Paris so he can attend school there. Jean-Claude, already a brilliant scholar, a young man brimming with French *politesse, savoir-faire, croyance en soi* mixed inevitably (every good thing has its down side) with French arrogance and the intolerance of youth, is what we call in plainest English the apple of his mother's eye, and to his stepfather something of a pain in the neck.

Before these recent departures, however, Otto and I talked a great deal about our shared past, a subject which doesn't altogether please Louise (I dream of composing a popular song with the refrain "How can I please you, Louise?"), in part because what interests us most occurred before she was born, or when she was just *une jeune fille*, and more because so much of it revolves around the subject of Samantha Conlan whom Otto described, all those months ago, as the love of his life.

"I begin to think she is the love of both your lives," Louise said one night as we were getting ready for bed. I was standing at the open window looking over the moonlit olive groves sloping away to the river, and the maquis-covered hills rising beyond, catching now and then the flicker of a bat across my line of vision, and struggling with the thought that in human affairs we pray for peace, good order and material comfort, and then suffer either guilt or boredom (or both) when the prayer is granted. At this moment for me it was guilt. Such comfort so effortlessly achieved! Such excess! How had I lived through two thirds of the appalling century just concluded without once dodging a bullet, hearing a bomb explode, experiencing hunger, being execrated for my skin-colour or persecuted for my penile surgery?

"I think she is the one you should have married," Louise persisted.

We had eaten that evening in the wall-enclosed courtyard of an ancient farmhouse, now a restaurant. My choices had been *magret de canard*, preceded by a goat's cheese salad, and followed by *tarte aux pommes*, with wine from the local vine-yard; and as I turned from the window to look at her it seemed to me that Louise, glowing with good health and high spirits, deserved a better fate than marriage to an aging writer burdened with a sense of history.

"You are very beautiful," I said, meaning it.

She was quiet for a moment before she said, "You are clever at evasions, *mon Oncle*," (I've twice been taken for her uncle, a famous playwright) "but I think what I said might be the truth."

And yes it might be "ze truce", if only we could ever know what that was. Certainly there has been a deal of nostalgia in my talks with Otto. Frankness too, so I have even been able to hint to him, and finally to admit, that when he first got in

157

touch with me in Auckland I hadn't the least idea who he was.

Otto's memories of Sammy are particular and detailed. In the short time they were together he heard a great deal about her life, and remembered it. There's a German thoroughness about him. The records, memorials, mementoes of what he has cared about in his life are preserved and filed in good order – and uncluttered, because what has been unimportant he discards. So he's usually able to find what he wants – and what *I* want.

During these months of writing I've also had my occasional exchanges of emails with Sam herself (she's now Samantha, I notice) as a source of information; but I haven't wanted to overuse this for fear of alerting her to the fact that I'm writing about her – something that might well alarm her and cause her to fall silent. But since arriving in France it has seemed a good idea to let her know that Otto and I have discovered one another, that I'm here with him, and that of course we find ourselves talking about the past. She seems amused, and not unwilling to answer an occasional question which I send as if it's just something that has come up between us in conversation. One thing that has surprised me, and surprised Otto too, is that she seems to have so little recollection of her *Secret History of Modernism*. "Nothing came of that," is what she replied to my question. "It never got off the ground."

Otto shook his head when I showed him her message. "She put so much work into it," he said. "I have a complete chapter somewhere. I'll dig it out for you."

Each morning I set off walking along beaten clay lanes between freestone walls, through vineyards, small orchards, olive groves, fields of wheat and fields of sun flowers, until I come to a rough path into woods – down past a chateau and mill-house, over a stream, climbing again until I come out at the edge of the town. At the internet shop I receive and send emails, and I'm usually reading in the shade of the *Place aux Herbes* and drinking coffee when Louise, or Louise and Otto together, arrive to join me, having come by car (they are not walkers in the summer heat) and parked somewhere on the *périphérique*.

But now for the moment I'm alone in the house, and yesterday I read the chapter of Sam's *Secret History* which Otto, as promised, had found for me among his files. He thinks there's little or nothing in it that Sam invented – that somehow she got all this information out of published sources or from manuscript letters and journals. I pointed out that most of it takes place in Hammersmith. Didn't that suggest she was setting it there because she'd lived there and knew the district?

Otto thought not. "I think it's set in Hammersmith because that's where it happened."

The chapter is called "Only Connect!" – a phrase taken from E. M. Forster's novel *Howards End*. It begins, in a street not far from the Hammersmith Bridge, around midnight some time in June 1917, and two people, T. S. Eliot and Katherine Mansfield, are walking away from a dinner party which neither has enjoyed. He is shy and darkly handsome, and she will later refer to him as "French polish Eliot". She is wary and darkly beautiful, and he will later describe her as "a very dangerous woman". Eliot has a wife, Vivien (usually Viv), whom everyone considers "mad"; Mansfield has a husband, John (usually Jack), whom nobody much likes; but each of these encumbrances has been left at home.

At the dinner party Mansfield has felt sorry for Eliot because she knows he's American, and she has observed him wincing when their host was being rudely John-Bullish about the United States. And Eliot has felt sorry for Mansfield because he knows her brother was recently killed in France, and he has noticed her flinching when one of the guests, the young officer-poet Robert Graves, talked of bringing some of his frightened men back into battle at the point of his revolver. Katherine's sympathy for Tom Eliot the American in Britain springs partly from her own uncomfortable sense of being a "colonial" there. Tom's sympathy for Katherine the grieving sister springs partly from his own distress at the death of his friend Jean Verdenal, killed at Gallipoli . . .

So the chapter goes on, working all the time to find parallels and make connections. Each of these two characters has slightly disguised an original accent. Both are associated with the Bloomsbury set, the "*in*-group" of that time among the literary young in England; but as non-English, neither is quite *of* it. Both are twenty-eight, born within ten days of one another. Eliot's pseudonym at this time, used in magazine articles and sometimes in his letters, is *Apteryx*, Latin name of the flightless bird, the kiwi, "unique" (Sam writes) "to Mansfield's home country New Zealand". And if the Bloomsbury Group are already talking about "young T. S. Eliot" this is partly because Katherine, who reads very well, recently read to them his poem "The Love Song of J. Alfred Prufrock", causing "a minor sensation".

But now the connections are spread wider. The place where Katherine read Tom Eliot's poem was Garsington, home of Lady Ottoline Morrell. Visiting Garsington while on leave recovering from war wounds, the poet Siegfried Sassoon has decided he must make a public statement against the conduct of the war. Ottoline Morrell is the mistress of Bertrand Russell, who has taken a brave pacifist stand, and at the Hammersmith dinner party Robert Graves, anxious that his friend Siegfried might be court-martialled, has spoken angrily against Russell's influence.

Tom Eliot and Katherine Mansfield have said nothing during this outburst, and now we learn what lies behind their separate silences. Katherine has had a flirtation with Bertie Russell which aroused Ottoline's jealousy and went right to the brink of an affair. Tom has been helped by Russell, who let the newly-married Eliots share his London flat, gave them money, and even, when Viv's "nerves" were bad, took her on a holiday to Torquay where he may have seduced her.

As for Sassoon's intended public statement which was giving Robert Graves such anxiety, Katherine could, if she chose, have quoted it word for word, because Sassoon, at Ottoline's suggestion, has brought it to Katherine's husband, Jack Murry, and the two men have gone over it getting the wording exactly right.

Sam's chapter ends with a scene that takes place before the Hammersmith dinner party. Siegfried Sassoon and Jack Murry have finished going over the statement of protest and, together with Katherine, they walk down towards the Thames. It is a beautiful night, the sky full of stars and searchlights, and Katherine silently reflects, as Jack goes on at length about how the carnage in France is "tearing him up" and "wounding his soul", that the war has driven them all, belligerents and pacifists alike, into falsity and even madness.

"Nothing seemed real to her," Sammy concludes, "not even her own feelings."

*

Last night, after reading Sam's chapter a second time, I slept soundly until the early hours of morning when I dreamed that I was in the foyer of what used to be – before I had in-laws to stay with – my favourite hotel in the Latin Quarter of Paris, the Récamier. Katherine Mansfield was there – in fact it seemed we were together. She'd told me in complete confidence that her name was really Kath Romancefield, and that she'd changed it to distance herself from her family, the Beauchamps. I could see through the windows the church and the fountain of the Place St Sulpice, so I thought this must be the hotel I remembered with such pleasure, but if it was the interior had been changed and there was a different *patron* behind the desk.

To Katherine I said, "This is the Récamier, isn't it?"

"No," she said. "It's Astoria."

I laughed, and the laugh woke me. I turned to see if Louise was awake, wanting to tell her that I'd had another of my word dreams, then remembered that she was in Paris.

I got out of bed, went to the window and pushed the shutters open. After a minute or two a car's headlights appeared, far away, a blade slitting lengthwise the black ribbon of the highway. The sound swelled and faded as the blade went through on its way to Remoulins. In the almost-silence that followed I imagined I could just make out the faint echoey dialogue of the river with the high bluffs of rock it flows through. First light would soon be breaking over vines and olives.

THIRTEEN

I Smell the Blood of an Englishman

"NOTHING SEEMED REAL TO HER, NOT EVEN HER OWN feelings." Sam wrote this of Katherine Mansfield. But was it what she herself felt at that time?

In London winter was on its way in and the decade of the fifties was on its way out. A hovercraft made its first crossing of the English Channel. Sputniks went over. There was an election which Supermac, with his "You've never had it so good" slogan, won hands-down. Those of us, the young of the Left, who worried about the treason trials in South Africa, the future of Rhodesia and Nyasaland, the Cold War with its nuclear menace, were dismayed. How could this have happened? We had short fuses, lacked the long view, and everything mattered frightfully.

The days grew shorter. A smoky fog-mist hung about the streets. Across the wide parks everything dissolved, "melted into air", as the trees turned orange-brown and shed their leaves, slowly at first, then with gathering determination to be done with it, to have it over, that thing which had been summer and had run its course. At times there was an almost golden glow over everything, like an ache of nostalgia, a regret that was not unpleasurable, and I went about inwardly murmuring the Gerard Manley Hopkins poem that begins:

> Margaret are you grieving
> Over goldengrove unleaving?

or slapping my hands, cross-armed, against my shoulders and chanting Ezra Pound's variation on an Old English song –

> Winter is a'comin' in
> Loudly sing *Goddamn!*

Darkness began to assert itself, arriving early and staying late. Chestnut sellers set up their braziers on the pavements of Piccadilly. In Oxford Street the Christmas lights went up and came on, and Sammy and Rajiv and I huddled inside our coats and scarves in Lyons Teashops, Kardomah Coffee Houses, student refectories, fingers wrapped around thick cups. We were short of money – I was certainly, and my two friends, despite their sources of help from home, seemed so too. There was a shortage of sixpences and shillings which half the inhabitants of the city kept for their gas meters. I used Sam's hairpins to pick that small padlock. The landlady, collecting the contents, was surprised how little gas I used. I was surprised it didn't occur to her that I might be recycling my shillings.

Sam had lost her job on the famous weekly. Marx Maclaren had sacked her; but I thought she'd wanted it, invited it. Her *Secret History of Modernism* was languishing and she was keen to get back to it. Also she wanted to be available whenever Freddy Goldstein was free to see her. Outwardly she was the same – clever, cheerful, talkative – but I knew her well enough to see, just below the surface, the uncertainty, anxiety, restlessness of one who was in love and the love was only imperfectly requited.

Marx liked Sammy and liked to tease her as an Aussie. She

didn't mind, so long as she could do the same to him as a Scot. She didn't understand, or couldn't accept, that this was not quite a two-way street. Marx was claiming a sort of *droit de seigneur*. If he imitated her accent that was OK. No harm was intended. If she imitated his, that might be impertinence.

Marx would sing, "Is 'e 'n Aussie / is 'e Aussie / is 'e 'n Aussie / is 'e, eh?"

But when Sam responded by singing, "Scots who ha' wi' Wallace bled / Scots whom Bruce hath often led", Marx tended to frown and register it as "cheek".

It came to a head over Christina Stead. Marx complained that her reviews came in "late, long, and lazily written", and he told Wilma Marienbad, loudly so Sam would hear, that he'd done a heavy copy-editing job on her that would "send her a signal". Christina Stead, it seemed, began to correct the proof, accepting the cuts but returning punctuation and word order to what she'd first written. And then, in what must have been an explosion of impatience at finding words as well as word-order changed, she scrawled across it, IF YOU PREFER YOUR COPY EDITOR'S PROSE TO MINE, *PLEASE* – GET HIM TO WRITE THE REVIEW!!!!

This seemed to please Marx Maclaren. It suited him very well. By now he'd persuaded himself he'd only taken on "the awkward and arrogant One" (as he called her) to please Australian Sam, and would now be rid of her. He wrote a stinger in reply – not a single angry sentence dictated off the top of his head, which was his usual response when opposed. This was carefully composed, referring to the novelist's "indifference to deadlines and casualness about limits on space", which "sorted ill" with her "grumbling about remuneration and requests for payment above the usual rate".

It was just on five – the hour when the office closed. Marx called Sammy to his desk and gave her the letter, hand-written, to be typed.

"I'll do it first thing in the morning, shall I?" Sam said. She was wanting to get away quickly because she thought there was a chance of running into Freddy, but only if she left sharp on the hour.

Marx said he wanted it done now.

"Are you going to wait and sign it?"

"I am."

"Isn't it too late for the post?"

"Just do it," Marx insisted.

She went back to her desk and read the letter. Its rudeness surprised her and made her angry. So did being "kept in". There was no chance now of seeing Freddy. The office was emptying. Marx was still at his desk, Wilma at his side.

The clack of Sammy's keys accentuated the deep silences when she sat staring at the text. Marx stayed at his post, perhaps guessing that she was taking her time, punishing him. The sinister Wilma leaned away from him into her larder-drawer and nibbled. At last Sam took it to him.

He began to read, then stopped. "This is not what I wrote."

"I corrected your spelling," she said.

He blinked and looked again at the text. "What spelling?"

"And your punctuation."

His face was hardening into anger.

She said, "And one or two words that didn't seem quite – you know? – right."

He put the letter down. "D'you think this is smart?"

She met his eye, not speaking. He said, "Get your things and leave."

"You mean . . . ?"

"I mean don't come back."

Wilma Marienbad said, "We have your address do we? We'll post your final cheque."

Sam swooped towards her. Wilma cringed away as if she was going to be hit. Into her ear Sam breathed, "There's a crumb on your whiskers."

In her last glimpse, from the door, of Marx MacLaren's face, she saw a look of surprise, and perhaps disappointment. Marx, she'd noticed, didn't like things to happen by accident.

So she was back with us at the British Museum, where Rajiv was now confidently into his stride with the work that would one day be *W. B. Yeats and the Deeps of the Indian Mind*. My own work was not going well. For some weeks I'd given almost all my time to writing the novel about the young man who was not unlike myself, and the young woman who, like Samantha Conlan, was in love with a survivor of the Holocaust. Unlike the real Sam, however, my Sam character got over her obsession with her Jewish lover.

There, of course, lay the problem. My novel was wishful. There was not a feeling of fictional truth about the young woman's transference of affection from the Freddy-figure to the Laszlo-figure. It was something I wanted to happen, but it wasn't something my imagination could make real to me.

There was one particular scene in which this transference was represented. The young couple – the Sam-character and the Laszlo-character – drive towards Southampton intending to see her Jewish lover disembark, but they never get there. They stop to climb a little hill and find a view over the countryside. They slip, roll down like Jack and Jill, entwined in one another and lost in the fragrances of spring flowers and crushed grass. They fuck (that word wasn't used – but the fact of it was clearly intimated) and afterwards lie watching a skylark rise from the hill and climb, "pinning its notes on the blue page of the sky".

Lyrical. Nice in it's way; but wrong. Not believable.

And yet, why not? – that's what I asked myself. Was it unbelievable because that fuck, and what followed from it in the novel, hadn't happened? Or because *I*, Laszlo Winter, couldn't believe in it? Was I failing as a writer because I was failing at life? I went over and over this question, suspecting that the fault was not in the writing but in myself. Yet how could I change? I could change the words on the page, but I couldn't infuse them with a belief which I lacked – a belief in myself.

Wearily I turned back to my Shakespeare studies.

I say "wearily", but the resilience of the young is extraordinary. Soon I was hooked again, though now my focus shifted. It was Shakespeare himself I was interested in – the man, the mind, the personality. So little was known about him, but I felt he was there in the writing, out of sight like Polonius behind the arras. He was behind the language, but *in* it too. Previously I'd been exploring and writing about his circumstances in the theatre and how these might have influenced what he put into his plays. But I wanted to get nearer to the real man, and what better route to take than through the sonnets, the most personal and potentially revealing things he had written?

I read and re-read those poems. At first they seemed obscure, then very obscure, and then impenetrable. They weren't like other "difficult" poems of that period. With John Donne, for example, or Andrew Marvell, when you'd

unravelled grammar and syntax, and picked up by hard work –
your own or some other scholar's – the contemporary refer-
ences, then everything fell into place. But with Shakespeare's
sonnets there was more than "meaning" needed explanation.
It was the human situation behind the writing that remained
unexplained. I wrestled with those 2154 lines, reading them
in sequence, reading them randomly, saying one or another
sonnet over to myself from memory – in bed, in the bath, in
the tube, in the concert hall when attention strayed from the
music, even at a football match (Rajiv and I had become Spurs
fans). Always I was trying to take the poem, and myself, by
surprise so that some new understanding would suddenly
come to me.

All this was combined with learning as much as there was
to know about the facts and circumstances of Shakepeare's life
during the early 1590s. It became an obsession – hard work,
but welcome because it took my mind off the things that were
unsatisfactory in my life, things I couldn't manage.

It was some time before Heather returned from Bristol.
When she did she seemed quiet, subdued. There were no
more headlong rushes on the landing and the stairs. It was
Harry Pulsford who told me her mother had died. The
mother had been persuaded she should have a hysterectomy
and had died under the anaesthetic before even the first cut
had been made. The family were told she must have had an
undetected heart condition but Heather was oppressed by a
feeling that a mistake had been made and the truth was being
concealed from them.

I took her flowers, talked consolingly (I wasn't good at it,
but did my best), gave her a hug – several hugs. She seemed
glad of that. We were friends again, but a space between us

had been restored by absence and by what in the meantime had happened to each of us. I could tell she wanted it that way, and it would have been insensitive – and also self-defeating – to try to cross it. The YoungAnimal-self watched her on the landing and remembered what we had done together; but the SensitivePerson-self kept him in check. "What you have in the hand is best," Rajiv said when I grumbled about my life. I'm sure he didn't mean it was more pleasurable, only more manageable, causing less interruption to life and work.

I don't know how many days or weeks I worked on Shakespeare's sonnets, always finding them more not less difficult, before first one revelation about them, and then a second, occurred. The first was just the recognition that the two sets of sonnets, the ones addressed to Shakespeare's patron, and the ones to his mistress, had been separated only for the purpose of making a book, and belonged together, covering exactly the same short period of the author's life. The other was much more radical. It was a recognition of the nature of the relationship between Shakespeare and his patron.

It came to me first in the form of a single word: *duress*. I was walking around Russell Square to catch the tube and the word stopped me in my tracks. In my head, as I applied what I meant by it first to one sonnet that had seemed obscure, then to a second, a third, a fourth, the problems seemed to vanish.

My excitement was huge. I felt like a detective who had all at once cracked a difficult case, and I was eager to tell someone. I thought of turning back and looking for Rajiv; but I could hear him in my head, saying in his on-rolling, rolling-on way, "Yes yes Laszlo I am sure what you are saying may be right but vere is the spiritual dimension for goodness sake?"

So I kept walking, past the tube station and on until I came to Sammy's flat in Doughty Street. I rang but there was no reply. I stuck a note under the street door saying Please Call Me, and headed back to the Russell Square tube. I thought of Margot, who knew this subject almost as well as I did. But there was always a darkness there – either because I was convinced I'd been right about her and Mark, or because I was in a mood to think I might have been wrong. In any case she was in Oxford and I wanted to talk to someone now, not tomorrow or next week.

So I arrived back at my bed-sit in a state of excitement and frustration. When I heard Heather on the stairs I rushed out to her. "There's something I have to tell you," I began.

She was unlocking her door. I didn't wait to be invited but went in with her. "It's about Shakespeare," I said. "I've made a huge discovery."

She shook her head, turning away from me as she put her parcels down and hung up her coat. "There's to be no more of that," she said.

"It's not what you think," I assured her. "I just I need to talk about it. It becomes so much clearer in my own head if I have to make it clear to somebody else."

It took a few moments but soon she was persuaded, I suppose because what I said was so impassioned and sincere. This was a crisis and she responded to my need.

"Fire away, then," she said. "I'll just get on with what I have to do here." And while I talked she set about preparing pasta and making a salad.

I explained that Shakespeare had a patron – the young Earl of Southampton – to whom the sonnets were addressed. So you could say he was in a fortunate position. But having a patron was also (and here I brought in the word that had triggered all this) a kind of duress. There were certain things he would be expected to say (the sonnets are full of flattery), and certain things that could not be said. So the feeling expressed was sometimes sincere and sometimes not, and to understand the sonnets you had to be able to distinguish. That's what made them so difficult.

Southampton was homosexual but kept it secret, even possibly from himself. He was under pressure from his family to marry and father an heir, but the lovely aristocratic girls who were wafted under his nose did nothing for him below the belt. Right from the very first sonnet, and on for the next sixteen, Shakespeare urged him to get on with it, accusing him of selfishness, of wasting his good looks by not replicating them.

But as you read on something else starts to strike you. Even allowing for the fact that men in Elizabethan times could be fulsome expressing love for one another, still there was something cloying and forced about the way Shakespeare went on about his patron. Southampton, I decided, had fallen in love with his poet . . .

"So Shakespeare was queer," Heather interjected, emptying a jar of pasta sauce into a pan.

"That's the trap," I said. "Oscar Wilde thought so, but everything contradicts it. You have to imagine yourself in Shakespeare's situation. An outbreak of plague has closed the theatres. He has a wife and family to keep in Stratford. And now he starts to notice Southampton's feelings for him. A rich aristocrat as an employer was great while he was pleased with you. But if you put a foot wrong you were in big trouble. Civil rights didn't come into it. You didn't have any."

Heather was tearing small pieces off the lettuce, testing it for freshness. "So the sonnets had to say nice things about the Earl."

"Nice things, yes," I confirmed. "But what if he wanted more?"

She had her back to the stove now on which the sauce was heating and water was coming to the boil. Her eyes were shining. I'd seen them like that before and knew what it meant.

I tried to explain – I did explain – how it seemed to me Shakespeare must have embarked on a policy of flattery at arms length, pretending all the time to think his boss was only interested in women, and urging him to find one. But then it got more difficult. The Earl began to tease and torment. First he made a great show of favouring another poet – probably Marlowe. Then he found a more tender spot: Shakepeare's mistress.

Heather was bringing out things to make a dressing, but this brought her around to face me again. "Shakespeare had a mistress?"

"You didn't hear at school about 'the dark lady of the sonnets'? Southampton went after her himself."

"You said he was queer."

"Queer – or bi. *And* an Earl. *And* very good looking."

Heather thought about it. "She would have known."

"Well, maybe she did. The sonnets give the impression he succeeded with her. Maybe that was just another kind of flattery. Whatever really happened, and whatever Shakespeare felt, he didn't complain. Instead of writing bitter sonnets about his employer, he wrote nasty stuff about the mistress. Said she was swarthy, ugly, promiscuous, manipulative . . ."

"He said all that about his girlfriend?" Heather was shocked.

"Yes, but that's where the cleverness comes in. If she was all those things, she was hardly a catch a handsome young aristocrat could boast about. And Southampton had only gone after her to nettle his poet. That hadn't worked. The poet didn't seem nettled at all, so the Earl dropped her."

"And that was what Shakespeare wanted."

"Yes, but you see why it makes the sonnets so hard to read. They weren't written for publication. They were written for the boss – and to *outwit* the boss. They're full of genius, and passion, but they're full of strategy too."

"Are you hungry?" Heather asked.

I shared her pasta and salad that evening, talking my way through the sonnets. I was still talking about them as we pulled off one another's clothes and fell into bed together. It was one of those violent fucks, a whole lot of stored-up lust explosively released. "Bang it into me," Heather said. "Hard. *Harder.*"

And that's what I did. Bang. Bang. Bang. With each thrust there was the slap of skin against skin and the thump of the bed rocking against the wall. She was being driven up against the headboard, her own head pushed around sideways as if her neck had been broken.

I stopped, thinking she might be hurt.

"Don't stop," she said. "It's OK." And then, gasping as I started again, "I'm quite robust, you know."

Strange how that word "robust" stayed with me. I could never hear it afterwards without thinking of the wildness of that fuck, and Heather using it to describe herself at a moment when her head was at an alarming angle and her whole body jolting and bucking on the bed-springs. I thought of it as the *mot juice*, and had to stop a moment because I was laughing.

Later when it was over and we'd recovered and were huddling under the covers, I felt a change in her. There was only briefly the warmth and companionship that would have been usual. A resentful note came into her voice. There was something negative she wanted to say but she couldn't bring it out. And since, intuitively, without having framed it into words, I knew what it was, I should perhaps have avoided asking. But I asked. What was the matter?

"Nothing," she said, but sullenly.

"You think I tricked you with that Shakespeare stuff. I didn't. I was desperate to tell someone."

She said she didn't care about that.

So what was the matter? I had to ask it again, and again she said there was nothing. But this time there were tears. I took her in my arms and settled down for what I knew might be a long sad story.

It was quite long, but what it amounted to was simple. Heather didn't like it when she enjoyed sex with me, because then she wanted to hold on to me. She knew, she told me, that I "didn't want her, except to fuck", and so when the sex was good what she felt afterwards was grief, and then anger. This was why she didn't want it to go on. She was becoming fond of me, and it hurt.

I told her I knew all that, understood it. It wasn't that I didn't love her, admire her, enjoy being with her. But (and I said it) "I'm in love with Sammy."

As I said it, I felt it. It swept over me. My own eyes filled with tears. What power words had! Speaking it to Margot had made it true. Speaking it to Heather made it real. And I remembered a story by Edgar Allan Poe, read during my school days, about two angels who bring whole stars and planets into being simply by speaking them.

Just a few days before Christmas Heather moved out. She was being set up in a flat in Chelsea by a rich businessman who was, she said, very old, very ugly, could hardly get it up, but at least he made her feel wanted. She said she would be bored, that she would send me her address and phone number, but she never did.

I saw her only one more time. It was in Regent Street, almost a year later. She was nicely dressed and in company with a bald, paunchy, significant-looking man in his forties wearing a good suit. This couldn't have been the old businessman she'd described to me, so she had either lied or moved on. He looked pleased with himself and with her. She had a spring in her step. As they came towards me I looked to speak. She sent me a small frown, a slight shake of the head, and I didn't greet her; but as they passed she must have seen me turning to watch them go. She slipped her hands behind her back and pointed to a gold band on the fourth finger. Then she gave a triumphant little shake of her neat round bottom.

I was pleased for Heather. Every young woman of those years (and almost every young man) wanted to be married. I missed her, and would have liked to tell her the news from the house – that Harry Pulsford was to marry the landlady, that there was a new and hairclip-resistant padlock on my gas meter coin box, that Mr Spiteri had swapped his room for hers and was learning to flush the loo, and that his room was now occupied by a prim and willowy young woman, Ethiopian-Greek, with the name Evrodiki and a face that belonged on an amphora or an ancient coin.

As for my sonnets theory which had put us back in bed together one last time: she would have found the news disappointing.

The day after my inspiration in Russell Square and my last rollicking fuck with Heather, I notified my supervisor that there would be "a slight change of direction" in my research. I was writing about the sonnets, and as soon as I had a chapter-length piece completed I would submit it for his approval. It didn't occur to me that he would be anything but pleased and impressed by what I was doing.

It took less than a week to get down a preliminary dozen or fifteen pages. I sent them to him and waited. Word came back quite promptly that he was ready to discuss them, and we met at a pub near UCL, the Marlborough. He sat with a pint on the table in front of him and my typescript clipped to a board on his knees. He was kind (he was always kind), but unconvinced, talking with a slow continuous shaking of the head which had the effect of signalling "No no no no", as background to whatever he said, like the tolling of a bell. What I had written was interesting, he said, but it wasn't scholarship. It was (and he repeated the word at intervals) *fiction*.

I went away puzzling over this, wondering whether scholarship and fiction were as different as he seemed to think. And then I gave it up. Even my supervisor, not knowing what he was doing, or what effect he was having on the future of my country's literature, had confirmed that I was a fiction writer. Once again late Shakespeare was abandoned in favour of early Laszlo Winter.

That Christmas turned into a two or three day reunion party at Castlenau Mansions, though Margot and Mark, briefly down from Oxford, didn't stay overnight. Rajiv and I dossed down in sleeping bags on the sitting room floor, as we'd done when we first arrived. Sammy shared a room with one of the permanent residents, Petra, a nurse from South Africa.

Dick Flinders came on Christmas Eve, and again two nights later, stoking his aromatic briar while he talked about his visit behind the Iron Curtain where, he assured us, "things are definitely on the move".

"Yes, tanks mostly," Sammy said; but Dick, who always made it clear that he knew much more than he was free to tell, smiled and didn't respond.

Sam came and went over the two or three days, sometimes sad and preoccupied, sometimes jolly, as if forcing herself to join in. I felt I should look after her and she liked that – cuddled up to me in front of the fire, let me bring her plates of food, pour her drinks. But when I asked what was troubling her she would tell me nothing, and I decided if I wanted to keep my position as friend and protector I should ask no questions. My reward would not be information, only propinquity.

Rajiv had been to Ireland – first to Dublin, then to County Galway to look at a medieval tower W. B. Yeats had bought and lived in for a time, and finally to Drumcliff Churchyard near Sligo to visit the poet's grave. To the assembled company he said it had all been "deeply re*varding*"; but in the night, as we lay side by side on the floor staring at the ceiling on which the yellow glow that came up from street- lights was cut across by the switch-shadows of bare trees, he told me there was one event in his Irish visit which had left him troubled – something he didn't like to talk about because British people would think it amusing and would laugh.

Alone in Drumcliff churchyard, standing at the poet's grave, Rajiv had taken his copy of Yeats's *Collected Poems* from his bag and, as a tribute, had read aloud an early poem called "Who goes with Fergus":

> Who will go drive with Fergus now,
> And pierce the deep wood's woven shade,
> And dance upon the level shore?
> Young man lift up your russet brow,
> And lift your tender eyelids, maid,
> And brood on hopes and fears no more.

There was another stanza, but somehow "the emanations" (I'm using Rajiv's word) were not right and he stopped. Perhaps, he thought, in death as in life the poet preferred his later work. So he turned to the back of the book and began to read "The Black Tower", a poem Yeats had written only a few days before his death.

"But this vas *vorse*," Rajiv said, his agitation as he told it making his accent more pronounced. "I had to stop. I couldn't go on."

He explained that the poem had a refrain which went:

> *There in the tomb drops the faint moonlight,*
> *The wind comes up from the shore:*
> *They shake when the winds roar,*
> *Old bones upon the mountain shake.*

"There was an invisible anger," he told me. "I felt it. And when I came to that refrain it got worse. The auras coming up from the grave – they were wrong. It got so strong I bolted. I never looked back. Just kept walking – fast – all the way back to Sligo. It must have been three or four miles, but

179

I felt you know as if I had been blown there by the *vind*."

I didn't laugh, and I'm glad I didn't. Many years later I was to read of new discoveries – or perhaps I should call them theories – about the great poet's burial. He had died in 1939 in the South of France and been buried first in Roquebrune Cemetery. Beside him was buried a certain Alfred Hollis who died in the same part of France on the same day. After the war, during which fighting between Italian and French forces had laid waste to parts of the cemetery, skeletal remains were dug up and taken by Irish warship for ceremonial interment in the sacred soil of Ireland – but there was now, this article explained, good reason for thinking they were not the right remains.

So Rajiv's mystical sense of an angry presence seemed to be confirmed. In the Irish grave, under the epitaph which the great Irish nationalist had written for himself, lay the body of an Englishman!

FOURTEEN

The Goldstein Story – 3

IT WAS THE NIGHT OF BOXING DAY. DICK FLINDERS WAS
holding forth about his trip to Moscow where "as a writer
he'd had the privilege" (about himself he was inclined to speak
like a committee) of meeting and talking with senior members
of the Soviet Writers' Union. We were spread around the
room in comfortable chairs and on cushions on the floor,
overfed, hung over, hoarse from too much talking and singing
and smoking, and not enough sleep. The three-day party was
coming to an end, and no one had the energy to ask Dick
what kinds of compromise taking favours from that particular
union at that particular time might involve. I was with Sammy
among the cushions.

I noticed her glancing at her watch. She was detaching
herself from me now, getting up, leaving the room. I moved
so I could see out into the corridor. She went first to the
bedroom she was sharing with Petra. A moment later I saw
her in her warm coat, leaving the flat. I got up and went
towards the kitchen as if to find myself another beer. Dick's
monologue rattled on. I doubled back to one of the front
bedrooms that had a balcony overlooking the street. The
night was misty, tending towards fog, each of the street
lights seeming contained inside a gauzy bag, like a large gas

mantle. The light came through and spread, but imperfectly. Everything was vague, soft-edged and shading away into darkness. From three floors up I saw Sammy come out into the street and turn right. She walked almost to the bridge, then stopped at the edge of the pavement and waited.

I could see clearly the near stanchion from which the steel suspenders curved out and down towards the centre of the bridge before rising again to the far stanchion which came and went as fog swirled up in irregular clouds from the river. There wasn't much traffic, and its sounds were muffled.

A car pulled up alongside Sam and she got in. It didn't drive away. A pale cloud continued from its exhaust. So they were in there, she and Freddy, with the engine running and the heater on, talking. Only talking, I decided, because they must have been visible from the pavement and from ground floor windows, and there was no move to a more secluded and shadowy part of the street.

I went to the kitchen, found myself a beer and a sandwich, returned to my watch. The fog swirled. Hooters sounded on the river. I shivered and my ears burned. But although my body reacted to the cold, it was as if I didn't feel it. What I felt was a drowsy, patient willingness to stand my ground, to wait.

The bang of Freddy's car door shook me alert again. Sam was walking back towards the entrance to the Mansions. Freddy cruised alongside her, leaned over to speak to her through the window, but she kept walking. At the entrance he got out, spoke to her across the top of the car. I saw the light shining down on his blond head, and remembered how Sam had described him as a *Mischling* Jew who looked the perfect Aryan, blond and blue-eyed. His voice came up

in the damp cold stillness. "Sam, don't do this to me. Please."
And the echoing bang as the front door crashed shut.

I waited for her at the door to the flat but she must have
stood a long time in the dark of the stairs, recovering. At last
she came in. Her eyes were dry but she didn't try to conceal
her agitation. "I'm going back to my flat," she said. And she
asked did I want a lift to mine.

I gathered up my things and we said our goodbyes. Her
Ford Popular was parked in a side street. In ten minutes we
were in Phillimore Gardens. I invited her in and she declined.
But then, as I stood in the street saying goodnight, she took
me by surprise, putting her hand over mine. "Would you do
me a favour, Laszlo? I feel . . ."

She swallowed hard. I thought she was going to say she
felt "unwell", but what she said was "shaky". She didn't want
to be alone. Would I spend the night on the couch in her
sitting room?

I galloped up the stairs, gathered a change of clothes, a book
or two and my current notebooks. Back in the street I found
her standing beside the car, leaning forward, one hand on
the top of the open door which was shielding her from the
street. She had vomited in the gutter. "That's better," she
said. She looked very pale under the street light. "Too much
Christmas," she said, more nearly cheerful now, and got back
behind the wheel. "Let's go."

I spent three or four nights at her flat in Doughty Street, the
perfect guest, thoughtful, helpful, undemanding, brotherly –
so hands-off and so . . .

I was going to write, blind and stupid! So many things
in life (one learns) are like Shakespeare's sonnets: you have
to understand what's said; but you also have to consider what

might possibly be *meant* by what's said, and how it might change with time and circumstance. She'd said she was "shaky". I took that to mean fragile. She'd offered me her couch. I took *that* to mean she was not looking for a volunteer to replace the unavailable man who was the cause of her distress.

We went for walks together, went to movies, had meals in restaurants (she paid, I did most of the eating), talked about our work, our families, our childhoods. She listened to my Shakespeare theory, was persuaded, thought my supervisor a very dull dog and that I should persist with it. When she spoke about her love affair with Freddy Goldstein, I gave her an edited parallel story of mine with Margot Derry so it might seem that we carried not dissimilar burdens of sadness. It was her turn then to give me comfort, not knowing that my lack of her, not my loss of Margot, was why I welcomed it.

When she decided it was time to write letters or work at something (I supposed it was her *Secret History*) I took out the notebooks I'd brought and pretended to busy myself with Shakespeare. What I wrote in fact was a record of our conversations, partly about her own life, partly about the Goldstein family, and in particular what had happened to Paul's brother Klaus and his wife and children.

Early in 1939 Klaus Goldstein had bought an escape for himself, his wife Clara and their children Ella and Franz. It hadn't been easy. He had gone to embassies and consulates in Berlin and at each had stood in a queue. After hours, a day, a day and a night, he had reached a desk, and always the same answer. His name would go down on a list – so far down he knew the crisis would have brought them to disaster or been resolved before the name of Goldstein got anywhere near the top. The idea of Cuba came late. If they could reach that island it was said the chances were good of getting past the United States immigration quotas.

It involved bribery and deception, as well as payments of "legitimate" demands to German officials and passport authorities. It cost Klaus's parents the last of their wealth; and in the end it was achieved. Klaus had new passports (stamped with the letter J) for departure from Germany, and though he couldn't get Cuban visas he had been given authorized entry permits. Better still, he had immigration quota numbers which guaranteed entry to the United States after a lapse of not less than three months and not more than three years.

When the documents were completed and the inflated fare paid, the sense of relief was immense. Klaus was no longer sad to be leaving the country he had loved and fought for and thought of as home. Anger had replaced sadness. There would be grief at abandoning his parents to a persecution which every day grew worse – but Paul had been right: what mattered was to save the children.

They were permitted to leave with ten Deutsche Marks each. In their large trunk Klaus packed two cameras, some crystal, jewellery, and (well hidden in a secret compartment) a small amount of gold. These he intended to sell in Cuba, since he would not be permitted to work there. Once that was used up they would have to depend on Jewish relief organisations to feed them until the door to the United States opened. After that would come employment, security, a new start.

On the night of 11 May, 1939, they said their farewells to Joachim and Beatrice, the four adults suppressing anguish and pretending they believed, and perhaps believing, that they would soon, or one day, be together again. Next morning Klaus and his family took the train to Hamburg to join 933 other refugees on the liner *St Louis*. On 13 May the ship set sail. Right up to the last there had been bullying, harassment and contempt. As soon as the ship cleared the harbour the atmosphere changed. The German captain, Gustav Schroeder, had given strict orders to his crew. This was a luxury liner with a standard of service to maintain. All passengers, without exception, would be treated with deference.

For Klaus and Clara, as for most on board, it was like jumping back ten years. It was a reminder of what, inch by inch, step by step, had been taken from them. Everything had been taken – money, possessions, rights, and finally dignity – until self-respect was a tattered remnant, and courtesies they would once have accepted without thought were almost a cause for embarrassment.

The ship docked at Cherbourg on 15 May. Four days later it passed by the Azores. The weather was good, the ship comfortable, the food superior. There was a swimming pool, a dance band. The children were entertained and the parents found friends. There were deck quoits, card tables, chess competitions, parties, concerts. When a Jewish service was held on a Friday evening in the ship's main lounge it was accepted that a blanket must be thrown over the bust of Hitler.

Everyone, Klaus noticed, laughed a lot, almost to excess. There was such a sense of relief on board – of escape, of waking from the nightmare. It was many days before a dark rumour began to circulate. The rumour was denied, repeated, contradicted, reasserted. The Nazi authorities (so the story went) were circulating photographs to the world of the most decrepit of the Jewish refugees (the oldest was 92) boarding the ship. In Havana a Nazi group were suggesting that "yet again" Cuba was being made to take in "undesirable vermin" and "dedicated communists". Within the Cuban Government some kind of argument was going on, had been going on even before the ship left Hamburg.

The pessimists on board believed the rumour. What Berlin was hoping for, they said, was yet another demonstration that countries which pretended to deplore Germany's rejection of its Jews did not want them either. That way, Jews would be shown to be everywhere undesirable, and all pretence to the contrary would be revealed as hypocrisy. Berlin would bring pressure on Havana. It would get what it wanted.

So the ship sailed on under a pale blue sky over a dark blue ocean that rolled enough to make its lordly presence felt but remained tolerant of their passage. On board, courtesy prevailed, the band played, the cooks offered top class meals, the bed linen was clean and white, but now fear sailed with them. Klaus lay awake at night below decks hearing and feeling the drum of the engines, the dip and slice of the bow that sent short sharp storms of spray across the bolted portholes. Yet even in those hours of the night when the darkest thoughts came, he found it hard to see how their escape could now be undone. If a trap was about to be sprung, what form could it take?

It came in the form of a declaration by the Cuban president, Laredo Brú. Entry permits issued to the Jews on board were declared invalid – cancelled, annulled. What became of Germany's Jews could no longer be Cuba's responsibility. Enough already had made their way to the island by irregular means. If there were valid visa holders on board the St Louis (there were in fact just twenty-two) they would be permitted to land. The rest would not. Word of this decree was signalled to the ship. It sailed on as if the message had not been received.

Early on the morning of 27 May, long before the sun was up, the *St Louis* entered Havana Harbour. Many of its passengers were on deck, having waited through the night. The pilot took control, the ship was guided in and dropped anchor. Those few not already awake were woken. Everything went ahead as for disembarkation. Breakfast was served. Health officials came on board. The passengers lined up, baring their wrists which were checked for signs of tell-tale rashes. Luggage was brought up from hold and baggage room and made ready for unloading.

But they were anchored just offshore, not tied up at one of the wharves, and there, throughout that day, and the next and the next, the *St Louis* remained, while messages went to and back between ship and shore, and from ship and shore around the world. Jewish refugees already in Havana hired boats and came to shout encouragement to friends and family lining the rail. The twenty-two passengers carrying full visas were allowed to disembark. The rest were advised to go away, find somewhere else.

The body of the 92-year old, a Professor Mendelsohn from Würzburg who had died on the voyage, was first taken ashore for burial, then returned to the ship when it was found he had not possessed a visa.

Each day the temperature rose and bad smells came up from the harbour water. The town, so close you might have felt you could reach out and touch it, could be seen going about its business. Some among the refugees fell into depression.

Fate, they said, which had treated them so badly in recent years, was playing its final cruel trick on them. Others became hysterical, angry, desperate, refusing to accept what was happening. Cuban police came on board to ensure there was order and that no attempts were made at unauthorized landing.

Ashore, and in newspapers and government offices around the world, the argument raged: what should be done? Some asked why Cuba should take more refugees while its wealthy neighbour, the United States, kept its quota so tight. Others asked what did the rights and wrongs of it matter? Compassion demanded that these people should not be sent back to persecution in Germany. In Havana, supported by his cabinet and by public opinion, the president declined to reconsider.

On the fourth day a Jewish man at the rail – a lawyer who had survived imprisonment in Dachau concentration camp – slashed his wrists with a razor and threw himself into the harbour. He was pulled aboard one of the small circling craft and taken ashore. Two days later, when the Captain Schroeder was forced to give up and sail away, the lawyer was still in hospital. He was the only non-visa holder to land in Cuba. His wife and daughter, refused permission to stay or even to visit him, had to sail with the ship.

Escorted out into international waters by the Cuban navy and by launches filled with armed marines, the ship with its nine hundred refugees, some wailing their grief aloud from the decks, others grimly silent, headed for Florida and anchored off Miami Beach. The captain had hoped the United States might relent, but again he was ordered to move on. He sailed "slow ahead" up the Florida coast, still hoping for a change of heart. Between the *St Louis* and the beaches coastguard vessels kept pace with him, watching for anyone who might try to swim ashore.

There was nothing to be done, nowhere to go but back across the Atlantic. While Nazi authorities in Hamburg were reported to be preparing to transport the returning Jews to concentration camps, the atmosphere on board was electric with anger, despondency and grief. The cruise liner had become a prison ship; and the seas, which had been benign on the voyage out, turned punitive on the return.

Day by day, hour by hour, pleading messages went out from the ship. Representatives of the passengers talked to the Captain. Desperate measures were suggested, including running the ship aground somewhere near Southampton, or setting it on fire.

But now, as the international clamour grew louder, there was another change of fortune. Stung by criticism, Washington offered to pay the costs if some other country or countries would take the refugees. Before the ship had reached Europe an agreement had been reached and broadcast to the world. Britain, France, Belgium and the Netherlands would each take a share of the nine hundred. Lots would be drawn for who would go to which country.

On 13 June, when Captain Schroeder read the news to the assembled passengers it was as if the immense relief Klaus should have felt, and did feel, couldn't be uttered for lack of breath. The cheers were mimed, the tears somehow squeezed. As his fellow-passengers wordlessly smote their brows, waved gaunt arms over their heads, hugged their children, or bent double as if in pain, Klaus felt he and they were acting in a silent movie. Something inside himself – faith, trust, the notion that anything at all, ever, could be relied upon – had died.

On 17 June the ship docked at Antwerp. Klaus and his family were among the one hundred and eighty-one Jews accepted by the Netherlands. From Antwerp they were taken by steamer to a quarantine station at Rotterdam where they remained for three weeks. Released, Klaus sold one of his cameras, two crystal bowls and some jewellery, and they took the train to Amsterdam. There a Jewish doctor colleague who had helped Paul spirit money out of Germany found them a small apartment on the edge of the suburb of Oosterpark, and helped them to find work in the local hospital, Klaus cleaning windows, Clara cleaning floors. Ella and Franz went to school and began to pick up something of the Dutch language. They lived frugally and saved, waiting and hoping that their American immigration quota numbers would come up. Two-and-a-half months after their landing in Antwerp, war was declared.

Klaus gathered in every scrap of war news, knowing that his family's future, perhaps even their survival, now depended on a German defeat. For many months little happened in Western Europe. But in the early spring of 1940 the real war began. German air and land forces swept all before them. In their victorious drive to the North Sea and the English Channel, they occupied the Netherlands.

The Goldsteins went into hiding. A Jewish relief organisation had supplied them with false papers to be used in an emergency, but they didn't dare show themselves in the streets. They were protected by an elderly couple, Catherina and Otto, Dutch Lutherans, who hid them in two tiny attic rooms reached by an interior ladder drawn up through the ceiling of one of two upstairs bedrooms of their house in central Amsterdam. What money the Goldsteins had – that and the small amount of gold brought from Germany – they gave to the couple. It was only to pay for the cost of keeping them, and was not enough even for that. Food was brought to them. Sometimes they came down into the upper rooms of the house to stretch and move about, but at first almost their whole life was confined to the attic. By daylight Klaus and Clara allotted the children times for lessons and times for play. They were not quite like real lessons, nor real play, but they gave a structure to the day. At night, without lights, Klaus and Clara slept, or lay awake remembering the past and dreaming of the future.

As time went by and their protectors became friends, Klaus and Clara were sometimes invited down at night and the four adults sat in the dark talking as well as they were able in their two languages, and listening to the radio for news of the war. They all longed for word of a German defeat but none came. When Ella, then later Franz, had birthdays, there was something like a party in the upstairs room, with a very small cake and a present, a children's book – not new – wrapped in coloured paper.

They had been in the attic a little more than a year when news came that Germany had invaded the Soviet Union. It was evening. Klaus lay on his back on the wooden floor while Clara, in the murmuring voice they had all learned to use even in anger, made up a bedtime story for Ella and Franz – a story of danger and escape that could be counted on to have a happy ending. Klaus stared at the steeply sloping ceiling, watched light fade from their tiny window, and for a while forgot his hunger as he conjured up the memory of an illustration he'd looked at often, in a childhood encyclopaedia, showing Napoleon's retreat from Moscow. Long lines of foot soldiers of that formerly glorious and invincible army – ragged, frozen, wounded, dying – dragged themselves through a pitiless winter landscape. Klaus felt an unfamiliar sensation in his face. He was smiling. The end of the nightmare might not come for a long time, but he felt sure now that it would come.

In the slow marking of time that followed, Klaus patched together the scraps of news that came from radio and newspapers, reading between the lines, separating truth from falsehood. Interpreting those bulletins was like learning a foreign language: he got better at it as time went by, even as the lies became larger and the truths more sketchy. Over the months he felt the surge of the Nazi invasion as it drove east. He felt it begin to falter, lose momentum, encounter at Stalingrad the ice wall of a Russian winter, the iron wall of peasant will, and begin to roll back. Meanwhile word-of-mouth stories came of Jews discovered in Amsterdam and deported east. No one knew where they were sent. None ever returned, and no messages came back.

That winter was particularly cold in the attic. In the night icicles formed under the roof, and there was often a skin of ice on the pail of water they kept up there. There were gas and electricity cuts. Food became scarce, and then scarcer. Yet every sign of the harshness of that winter pleased Klaus. He shivered and smiled, remembering the picture of Napoleon's retreat.

There was usually bread, but nothing else could be counted on now. Sometimes Catherina and Otto took an empty suitcase out by train into the country where a relative had a farm, and came back with sugar-beets or potatoes or white beans or carrots. If it was beets, they had beets for every meal; if it was potatoes, or white beans, or carrots, then that was the staple until they were gone. Often the old couple would bring back from the community kitchen, where their married daughter worked, a pail of what was called *schillen*, a soup made from peelings left by cooks for the occupying German soldiers.

Once, when they had not had meat for a long time, Otto brought home what the Dutch in those bad years called "roof rabbit". Catherina baked it, with some carrots and a gravy thickened with flour, and the four adults and two children had a feast. When it was eaten, and all the bones chewed and sucked clean, Franz said in German to his mother, "We know what roof rabbit is. It's cat." Clara looked anxiously at him and at Ella but they were smiling. Hunger had established new priorities.

One morning Otto called up to Klaus to drop down the ladder. He had been warned the whole street was to be searched. Everything, cellars and attics, cupboards and wardrobes and trunks, would be opened. The couple could not face asking the Goldsteins to leave; but nor could they face the consequences of being caught harbouring Jews. It was agreed that the Goldsteins would have to risk spending the daylight hours, until the search had been completed, in the streets and parks and cinemas of Amsterdam.

They were given a little money, spent a day in the city, returned to the house late and left again early the next morning. The first and second days passed and there was no search. These were wonderful days for Ella and Franz – to be at large, out in the streets, in the parks, in the open air – and would have been for the parents too except that they were on guard, anxious every minute.

On the morning of the third day they left, again when first

light was a faint glow in the eastern sky. They had reached only the end of the street when they were stopped by a German officer who asked in Dutch for their papers. Further down the street a detachment of soldiers with rifles were getting down from a truck, shouted at by a sergeant.

The officer stared at the papers, then at Klaus. "I believe these are forged," he said in German.

Klaus shook his head.

"Then why do you understand when I speak to you in German?"

"I speak it a little," Klaus said, imitating a Dutch accent.

"Do you speak German?" the officer asked the children.

They shook their heads.

Still in German he said to them, "So, little ones, you don't speak German?" Again they shook their heads. "Nein," said little Franz in a piping clear voice.

The officer ordered Klaus to drop his trousers.

"In the street?" Klaus asked. "In front of my family?"

The officer said they could go around a corner, into an alley. "No," Klaus said. "I am a Jew. Klaus Goldstein. This is my family." He named them, as if introducing them. "We are Jews," he said.

The officer nodded – it was almost a bow – looking at Clara and the children. His eyes were not hard, not vindictive. He turned to see how far away his men were. He might even have been about to tell the family to go away and stay out of sight, but another officer, wearing the uniform of the SS, was coming towards them.

The Goldsteins were taken first, overnight, to a police cell, then by train with ordinary carriages to what was called a "holding camp"; and finally, in one of the lines of cattle trucks that would one day be infamous, all the way to a concentration camp. They didn't know its name, nor even what country they were in – only that the journey had been a long agony. Klaus estimated there were at least fifty in the wagon. Days and nights passed without food or water or sleep, with nowhere to defecate but the floor, and nothing to do with those who collapsed, unconscious, or in one or two cases dead, but to leave them where they fell. Some women had brought food and drinks and at first shared them around. But as the journey went on they stopped giving; and soon there was nothing to give. By the end they were tottering with hunger, fear, physical and mental exhaustion.

Klaus tried to protect his children and console his wife; but already he had decided they must be going to their deaths. What else could be intended when the method of transport was so brutal?

It was very early morning, hardly light, when at last the train came to a stop, the sides of the cattle trucks were opened and the human contents spilled out. Search lights made everything harsh, black and white. They were in a very wide space – several acres – surrounded by high barbed wire fences with watchtowers. On either side rows of low huts stretched away out of sight. Straight ahead there was a complex of brick buildings with tall chimneys. Guards, some with rifles, others with fierce Alsatian dogs on leashes, herded the Jews into a long line and drove them forward to a point where the line was divided into two. Commands were shouted, and back in response came screams, wailing and shrieking. The dogs reared up on their leashes, snarling and biting. Rifle butts and short thick whips rained blows on heads and backs.

As they reached this place of tumult Klaus recognized that

healthy adults were being forced to the right, children, the elderly and the sick to the left. Two men, one a Gestapo officer, the other a man in the white coat of a scientist or doctor, were making the selection, while guards, soldiers, and others who were perhaps themselves prisoners, enforced it. The shrieks came mostly from parents separated from their children. "Don't worry," they were told. "The little ones will be well looked after." But the parents fought and shrieked and were beaten back, while the line to the left was forced on and away towards the brick building with the chimneys.

Klaus and Clara also fought and shrieked as Ella and Franz, crying, were torn from them. Klaus was beaten to his knees. For a moment he lost consciousness. Then, as he struggled to his feet, he saw that Clara had broken past the guards blocking her way and was with the children. She had a hand on each of their shoulders and was moving with the left line, but looking back. He saw she was glad to be with them, and he was glad that she was. The children would not die alone. In that last glance he always believed that she meant to say to him, "Stay alive. Be a witness for us."

FIFTEEN

"It was You, Laszlo. It was You."

KLAUS SURVIVED. HE WAS ONE OF THOSE VERTICAL STICK figures among the piles of horizontal ones when the death camps, with their unfinished business of wiping Jewry from the planet, were discovered to the camera lens and to the world. For many weeks and months afterwards he hovered between life and death. But he had not come so far, through so much, to be silenced now. Cared for, he lay still and quiet, waiting for a little strength to return, a little inner warmth, and slowly slowly these came back.

Klaus Goldstein denied that he was alive. From the moment his wife and children were taken from him, he insisted, his life was over. "I am a ghost," he said. "I am here only to bear witness."

He said little about how the intervening time had passed – only that no one survived in the camps except at the expense of others who did not. It was a sort of moral and psychic cannibalism, enforced by circumstances, requiring strength and will as well as luck. He would write to Paul, "Others died so I could speak. Except as a voice, I have no right to exist."

A year or so after the war ended Klaus made his way to Palestine. The British were still blocking ports, but the survivors, once their strength returned, were determined, and there were secret organisations to help them. When the time was right and the arrangements had been made he was put on a train to Athens. From there he was carried in the hot hull of a rusting freighter heading for Suez, to be transferred in the night to a fishing boat which brought him ashore, with others, into the port at Acre.

In the years that followed Klaus lived the life of an observing Jew, first on a kibbutz, then in Tel Aviv. He accumulated no wealth and few possessions, never remarried, and when opportunities presented themselves, spoke gravely and with dry-eyed dignity of the Holocaust and of what had happened to his family.

He exchanged annual letters with Paul, and later with his nephew. His messages were austere, somewhat formal, but with a simple authority. In the time when Samantha Conlan and Friedrich Goldstein were lovers Freddy had still not met his uncle, but he hoped – intended – that one day he would. In the meantime Klaus's distant presence existed as a moral force in his life. Through his wife, Ruth, Freddy had reclaimed his Jewish inheritance and had passed it to his son. He felt this as an obligation to his murdered aunt Clara, to his murdered cousins Ella and Franz, and to his grandparents Joachim and Beatrice who had also died in the gas chambers of Auschwitz.

I noticed during those days I spent in her Bloomsbury flat how little, and how randomly, Sammy ate, that she threw up sometimes and tried to conceal the sounds from me, and that if I mentioned it she brushed me off. It crossed my mind that she might be pregnant; but the vomiting happened at different times of the day, and even in the night, and since I'd always heard the nausea that came with pregnancy described as "morning sickness", I accepted what she said, that she "had a bug", or had overdone the eating and drinking at Christmas, or both.

Most of the time she seemed in excellent health – lively, affectionate, clear-eyed, but inclined to drop off to sleep, sometimes letting her head fall on my shoulder as we sat side by side on her couch listening to music or comedies or quiz programmes from the BBC. I don't know how long I might have lingered there, and what might have come of it. There was no suggestion I should hurry away, though at first she'd invited me only for a night. Could we, I began to ask myself, become flat mates?

That was my thought, which, as always, ran a long way ahead of my courage.

One evening when Sam was dozing and I was writing in my notebooks there was a buzz from the street. I went down. It was Harry Pulsford. A telegram had arrived for me from New Zealand. Marked URGENT, it had been lying for three days on the table under the mirror in the entrance hall at Phillimore Gardens. Telegrams in those days were sometimes greetings, but more usually they represented important news. Important *bad* news, most often. Harry had somehow got the Castlenau Mansions address, and from there had been directed to Sammy's flat.

I thanked him profusely and didn't invite him up. He must have been used to that, especially late in a fishy week. I watched him drive away in his white van with its Botticelli-style picture of a mermaid on a clam shell over the company name, "Fanshaw's Fish & Oysters".

The telegram was from my father. It asked me to "call

by phone as soon as possible". I was gripped by a feeling of anxiety. My father was of a generation and an income bracket that only made toll calls or took taxis when there was an emergency.

There was no phone in the flat, and long distance calls couldn't be made from public phones. You had to go to a special "Tolls" branch of the Post Office. You booked in your call and sat with others, waiting for it to go through, which might take an hour, or several hours.

It was Sammy who worked out the time difference. If the call went through too soon I would be waking my parents before dawn. I should let her prepare me a meal, let a little time go by, sit and talk to her over coffee or a glass of wine.

I agreed but found I couldn't wait. Couldn't sit still. I was anxious and had to be out of there.

OK she said. But first there was something she wanted to say to me.

She came up very close and looked at me in a way that I thought meant . . . But how could it? My body thought it did, but I told my body it was wrong. And in any case there was the telegram . . .

Sam's hands were on my upper arms. She was thanking me for what I'd done for her over Christmas – but even more in the days since Christmas. "You've been so patient . . ."

I could taste her breath. "I've loaded so much on to you . . ."

And then she stopped talking and kissed me. It was that kind of kiss, but violent, and her teeth cut my lip. I wiped my mouth and bolted.

I remember Mark Derry telling me that when he was a schoolboy, a natural talent at jumping but knowing next to nothing of techniques and training, he was entered for an inter-schools competition, and in the elimination round he was the only athlete to clear the highest jump at first attempt, so his chances in the final seemed better than good. That afternoon, waiting for his event, he lay very still on the grass thinking he was saving himself, preserving energy. He could see other jumpers running about in track suits (something he didn't have), exercising, doings high steps and springs, even sprinting, and he thought how foolish they were, wasting their strength. When the event began the bar was set first six inches lower than he'd jumped in the elimination round. Margot was in the stand. He'd told her about his success in the morning, and she'd come to see him win.

He missed all three attempts, and was eliminated.

In the years that followed a coach took over his training and he learned about warming up before an event, and how it is that cold muscles won't perform. Since that time he'd won certificates, medals, cups, titles; but of all his sporting memories what remained most vivid was missing those three jumps. He had wanted so much to win, and winning had seemed certain. The disappointment remained with him while the triumphs faded.

In some moods, when I look back over my life, I feel about that kiss at Sam's door as Mark felt about his schoolboy failure. Why did I bolt? What would have happened if I'd stayed?

It would be easy to invent explanations. For example, I now know that Sam was pregnant. I must already have guessed it, or half-guessed. So if she meant to take me to bed at that moment, would she then have said I was the father of her child? Or if, on the other hand, she had taken me to bed and afterwards told me that she was pregnant to Freddy

Goldstein, would I have felt trapped? How would I have looked at the prospect of becoming father to another man's child – especially one with that inheritance, that burden of ancient wrongs?

With thoughts of this kind, and adding further twists and complexities, I could easily (if I were writing fiction) construct a narrative path through a maze of guilts, subtleties and moral dilemmas. It could be wonderfully intricate, like a novel by Henry James. None of it would be true.

I bolted because I loved her, because it mattered so much, because I was shy and socially incompetent, because for once love took precedence over sex. My retreat was in its way a clumsy tribute, a primitive kind of decency. I wanted what she seemed to be offering so much I was afraid she might think that was all I wanted. Unfortunately, she could know none of this. She must have felt (I can see it now) that she'd offered herself and been rejected. And meanwhile I was too distracted by the news from home to sort out in my mind just what had happened at that dizzy moment, or make any effort to correct the misunderstanding it had created. All that, I must have thought, would come later.

My father had cancer. It had only just been discovered, and although for the moment it was not seriously affecting his life, he'd been told he had only six months to live. Nothing could be done. He didn't want to upset me or disturb my research and writing, but I was his only son and he would like to see me one more time before he died. He'd talked it over with my mother, reviewed what he called their "reserves", and decided if I could come, and wanted to, they would pay my return airfare. That way there would be a minimum of disturbance to work on my PhD, which he insisted mattered more than anything else. If it was going to make the slightest difference to my completing the degree, he would drop the idea at once.

It was a bold plan. In those days the cheap means of travel was by sea. Only the rich travelled by air – something I'd never done. So it was exciting as well. And of course it wouldn't interfere with my PhD – wouldn't have interfered even if I'd been doing it. He was going to die and he wanted to see me. I would go.

That night I dreamed about my parents' house. I'd dreamed more than once lately of the letterbox at their gate, full of uncollected letters. This time, among the soggy mail and advertising brochures were packets of meat. They were still cold and stiff from the refrigerator and I realized that my father had died and my sister was cleaning out the kitchen. My mother came on a bicycle, wobbling down the path through trees, the back carrier piled with newspapers. "I'm taking these to the Moronis," she said. "They turn them into money."

I held the gate open for her. She pedalled past me, turning into the quiet suburban street and out of sight beyond a tall hedge. Almost immediately I heard the bike crash down. Silence. I listened and heard the hedge stirring in the breeze. She groaned and began calling to me: "Laszlo, I'm hurt. Laszlo." I would have to go to her – didn't want to – and now came the thought, the recognition that this was a dream. If I exerted my full strength I could escape. I struggled towards consciousness like a non-swimmer in deep water, fighting to get out.

When I woke properly I was shocked at the dream-determination I'd felt to escape from my Mum's need of me.

Next day I called my supervisor and everything was arranged – even that my scholarship payments would continue while I was away. It happened in a rush. I continued to have disturbed dreams. Somewhere below consciousness I was trying to deal with the knowledge that my father was dying. On the surface all was practicality and urgency.

I flew by Pan Am Boeing 707 to New York, then on a night flight to San Francisco connecting with a morning one to Honolulu, but the connection was missed which meant a twenty-four hour delay. Bewildered and a day behind schedule at Honolulu, I remember seeing three nuns holding their wimples down in a breeze on the sweeping white curve of a concrete ramp, and feeling I was already in the future. Fiji came next – cane fields and jungle in the night – and then onward over those last turbulent fifteen hundred miles of the South Pacific by what was called a "turbo-prop" – not a jet, because there were no runways in New Zealand long enough to take them.

My dad had lost weight but that suited him. I thought he looked rather handsome, and even in quite good health, though he was beginning to have intimations (stabbing pains, dizziness) of what lay ahead. He'd been fit and active and liked still to walk quite long distances, which he would continue to do until the serpent within began seriously to bite. It was his idea that I should drive him to the Bay of Islands where he'd spent his childhood and where he'd often taken us for holidays. We would see the sights, do a little fishing if he felt up to it, go across to Russell in the ferry, eat out, talk about his past and my future.

And that was how it was, except that for me, apart from, or alongside, concern for Dad, and my sense of imminent loss, there was the excitement of seeing that region – "up North" – with fresh eyes. In my time away I'd forgotten the qualities of light and air, the way the semi-enclosed waters – harbours and gulfs – on that eastern coast seem to stretch away at eye level almost without a diminishing perspective, and the way the islands in them appear to float and to dream. I will resist the temptation to go on about these wonders and say only that my attachment, not so much to my country (though at the time I might have expressed it as a kind of nationalism) but to my home region, was confirmed. Whatever I wanted to do with my life it would have to be here.

It pleased my father that I was able to say so. I intended to tell him also that I'd come to recognize I would never make an academic, and that I wanted to give up the PhD and embark on some kind of life as a writer. In the timeless hours on the flight out I'd gone over this confession in my head. Remembering that favourite line of mine from *A Midsummer Night's Dream*, I'd imagined saying to him that my ambition was "to give to airy nothing/A local habitation and a name". There was for me such magic in those words, I thought he would see what I meant, would be persuaded, and pleased for me.

But my dear old Dad (and he was not so old – too young to be dying) had no feeling for poetry, none at all, and I didn't even try the Shakespeare line. In fact we had only begun to touch on my future when I recognized how wrong it would be to tell him of my intentions. He was so much a product of bad times, the idea of my not taking secure employment (with safe superannuation) would have upset him. I would reserve the truth for my mother, who would take it better, and might even live to see that it hadn't been such a bad decision.

So I let him think nothing in my plans had changed. Why should he not go to his death believing that I would have both superannuation and doctorhood, twin angels guarding the gates to a brilliant future?

But there were other moments when he offered advice that seemed not only right, but as if it came in answer to something I'd thought but hadn't said. Once, speaking after a silence that had lasted from the Waitangi Marae almost back to the Paihea Wharf, he said, "Don't let timidity get in the way of living, Laszlo. It's bold energetic people who get most out of life."

It struck with peculiar force, because in that long ambulant silence I'd been remembering Sammy's kiss, and how I bolted from it. "Yes, Dad," I said. "But you can't act beyond your own nature."

We can never be quite in a state of ease and equality with even the best of parents, whose slightest frown or least seriously intended correction may turn us in an instant back into the children we once were; but during those few days he and I got pretty close to it; and when the time came for goodbyes we said them as the conventions of the time required – "like men". The eyes were dry. (Tears would come later, but alone and out of sight.) And certainly there were no hugs. (We were not Americans.)

"Goodbye, son."

"Goodbye, Dad."

A firm handshake, a frank and manly meeting of blue-grey eyes. Coriolanus couldn't have done it better.

I got back to London intending to face Sammy like one of those "bold energetic people who get most out of life." I would tell her the truth about my feelings, wrench her away from her obsession with Freddy Goldstein. But no one answered her phone, no one came when I knocked at her door. I went back two or three times before I thought of Castlenau Mansions.

It was the South African, Petra, who answered the door there. Didn't I know? Hadn't I heard? Sammy had gone back.

"Back?"

"Home. To Australia."

"But why?"

Petra didn't think there was a why. "You know Sammy," she said.

I walked down to the tow path and stared at the water. In the days that followed I wandered daily by the Thames, disbelieving, believing, saying over to myself,

> The river's tent is broken: the last fingers of leaf
> Clutch and sink into the wet bank. The wind
> Crosses the brown land, unheard. The nymphs are
> > departed.
> Sweet Thames run softly till I end my song.

I wrote to her of course, but tentatively, and uncertain that I had the right address. There was no reply.

I think two years must have gone by before I had word of Sammy again. She was living in Sydney, the mother of a little boy, and had just married, or was about to marry, a lecturer in German at the University of Sydney.

Very recently, sitting by the pool talking to Otto Stiltz about her, I reminded him that when we talked in Auckland he'd said his marriage to her didn't last because when they met she'd been "on the rebound from a rebound". That seemed to mean there was someone between Freddy Goldstein and Otto himself.

He nodded, rather formal. "Of course."

"And that person . . . It was . . ."

He looked at me, frowning, surprised, uncomprehending. "You don't know? But of course you do. It was you, Laszlo. It was you."

SIXTEEN

"Not to Forget my History"

LOUISE AND I ARE BACK IN AUCKLAND. IT'S SPRING, blustery today, sending the last few scraps of white blossom flying from the plum tree and putting white caps on the waves of the Hauraki Gulf which we see from our front windows.

A reply has come from Sam . . .

But a reply to what? I have yet to explain.

I suppose we'd been back a week or ten days. The unpacking was done. I'd heard Louise's stories of Paris, of her mother, the ever-ailing Françoise, of her son, the never-failing Jean-Claude. She'd heard mine, mainly of writerly vexations and anxieties, problems with my lap-top, email failures and Muse-defections.

We were home, settled again. Louise's appetite for France, its people and culture, its language and landscape, was satisfied for the moment and she was in a mood to look out at, even to admire and enjoy, the knockabout wooden-house world of "ze souse seas" – to put up with its fresh air, shock her body in its clean cool waters, appreciate its good food, and give serious thought to (for example) new curtains for the sitting room, a new bed-cover for the guest room, a bright yellow non-stick shower-mat for the en suite bathroom, a matching red toaster and coffee pot for the kitchen, some pot plants for the seaward patio, a CD of that wonderful singer we heard in . . .

I was glad of this upswing in her mood, and with the optimism that never quite deserts me I believed (and who's to say — yet — that I was wrong?) it would last. Louise's highs, however, were not inexpensive. I would need to publish another book.

Meanwhile my writing had come to a dead stop. This I told myself was for lack of answers to certain crucial questions, for lack of detail — but really, I think, it was because of a lapse in confidence. It was, as these things are, mysterious, inexplicable.

I decided I would email Sammy a long letter. No more of these clever exchanges of one sentence questions and one word answers. Put my cards on the table. Let her know where I was, where I'd been, that I'd got on well with her "Stiltskin", that I was "writing about those far off days" (I would put it like that) and needed her help.

For quite some time there was no reply and I began to think she must have climbed back behind the barricades. The game was up, it was the end of the road, my goose was cooked, she wasn't coming to the party.

The buds on the plum tree put out pale points and opened into miniature flowers of purest glossy white. Soon the petals were snow-showering down replaced as they fell by the extravagant green of new leaf. The kowhai at the gate came into flower, and one morning Louise picked a troika of blooms and placed it on my desk with the message, "*Voilà, pour toi, Laszlo — trois cloches d'or. Travaille bien, mon amour!*"

"Here for you, Laszlo — three golden bells. Work well, my love!" It was such a nice, such a Gallic, gesture, but it only increased her *amour*'s anxiety. How could he tell her that he wasn't working at all?

Then at last came Sam's reply – a long one, a helpful one.

She was living in Rushcutters Bay, which has been her home for the past twenty years. She was, she said, glad to answer my more detailed questions, and would help me all she could, if I would be willing to do one small thing – she hoped it would be small – for her. But she had one slight anxiety. I would not be writing – writing *explicitly* – about her, about us, about our friends and friendships and love affairs, would I? Someone had sent her Dick Flinders's "memoir" and she'd been relieved she hadn't known him better, because she didn't feel she wanted to find herself recorded as an *episode* in someone's – anyone's – life.

Have no fear, I told her in an over-eager reply. Fiction is my trade, not gossip. Of course "for a writer" (it was an excuse I'd never liked, but I resorted to it) everything was grist to the mill. But "everything" comes out changed, transformed, unrecognisable. I told her about a novel I'd written (had she perhaps read it? – but I guessed not) in which a character who runs a café has his laundry done by a small company called the Magic Bagwash, which has on its logo, and on its delivery van, the motto "Everything Comes out White".

"Fiction's like that," I told her. "Everything comes out white. You need have no anxiety."

She seemed to accept this. She promised to help.

I'd been telling myself I was writing a "memoir", and now I'd told Sammy it was fiction. Which was true, and had I lied to her? I suppose in a way I had, except that the difference between the one and the other was no simple matter. Did changing people's names make autobiography into fiction? Did real names – Laszlo Winter, or Dick Flinders – make autobiography less fictional? There would be time, I decided, to think these problems through, but it couldn't be now. Now I had to be intent on completing the job. I had Sammy's permission to ask her the harder, more personal questions. Maybe I wouldn't need to ask. Imagination, after all, is a master-key, and all (all!) you need, in order to use it, is confidence and intelligence. Confidence was what her reply had given me. Intelligence I had enough of – or if not, there was nothing to be done about it. I could move forward now. I could also move back and make revisions.

It was spring, Louise was happy (she was shopping), Sam was an email away, and I was in business again.

On that night just after Christmas when Sam met Freddy Goldstein and sat with him in his car, she knew, though she hadn't been tested, that she must be pregnant. She'd resolved she wouldn't tell him. She would give him this one last chance to leave his wife for her, without any reason other than love. She knew he would refuse. Then she would tell him their affair was over and say goodbye. It wouldn't be the first time she'd said goodbye to him, but it would be the first time she'd enjoyed saying it.

Her mind was clear – almost clear. She knew that she wanted Freddy to refuse her, and that she wanted it because somehow, in the turmoil of recent weeks, her love for him, which she'd once thought inextinguishable, had fluttered like a weak flame and gone out. Her feeling of being bound not merely to the man but to the history he brought with him, had exhausted itself. It was as if she'd been intent on mothering, or fostering, the whole Jewish race; as if she'd wanted to atone for what her sort had done to his sort. This perception of another motive for her love than love itself shocked and embarrassed her. She felt she'd caught herself out in egotism, self- importance, self-deceit. Had she really seen and known the individual, the unique, Freddy Goldstein? Or had she seen in him, and known through him, only the sad history of his race?

What she longed for now was escape. She wanted kindness, patience, equality and good fun. She was sick of passion, especially her own; tired of the turbulence and confusion that went with it. She wanted a friend – a Laszlo Winter kind of friend.

But she had that kind of friend. She had Laszlo Winter.

She decided she had allowed herself to be caught up in categories. Freddy had been her lover, Laszlo her friend. Why should those positions remain fixed for ever? Why should Laszlo not be the lover? And why (this was the kind of fantasy with which Sam entertained herself in bad times) should Freddy not be rocketted into orbit like the Russian dog Laica; or sent across the southern polar ice with Sir Edmond Hillary. It wasn't that she wanted Freddy dead; but it gave her satisfaction to imagine him gone somewhere extravagantly far away – even gone from the planet. That she was bearing his child didn't matter. It made the idea of his absence even more attractive. Anything she owed him, and owed the Jewish race, was growing inside her. The debt was paid.

So in the car that night they had one of their rows – a big one, a ding-dong. A lot of it centred on whether Freddy slept with his wife, and whether he enjoyed it. In the past, and without asking the question, Sammy had managed to persuade herself that either he didn't sleep with Ruth, or that if he did, he didn't enjoy it. Now it had occurred to her that this was naïve. She remembered how he'd told her in Canberra about his father and the Latvian flower-seller; how Paul had become more than ever his wife's lover at night while he had Marthe Borowska by day. How could she have listened to this, Sammy asked herself, and not seen that Freddy had been speaking of himself? He had even said it: "You are my Latvian flower-seller."

Now she demanded to know: he slept with Ruth, didn't he? Made love to her?

Grudgingly, Freddy acknowledged that he did – though he managed, without stats., to give the impression that it didn't happen often.

And did he enjoy it?

Badgered, refusing at first to answer, or to give an answer that made any sense, Freddy said finally that it was difficult not to enjoy an orgasm.

That was only a beginning. The row built from there. On a scale of 1 to 10 Sammy rated it 9.5. Only the cold, and the restricted space which prevented throwing and hitting, cost it the final half point. They'd had rows like it before, and no doubt Freddy Goldstein thought there would be more. He didn't know she meant it when she said it was all over between them. She'd said it so often. But she did mean it.

"Please don't do this to me," he begged over the top of the car as she marched into Castlenau Mansions slamming the door. Later, when he found that all access to her was denied, and finally that she had gone back to Australia, Freddy would feel the pain. He had loved her, as he didn't doubt his father had loved Marthe Barowska; but like his father, Freddy loved his wife and child as well, and knew where his first duty lay. He would grieve, he would suffer, he would long for her, he would weep. But he would also be relieved. Not knowing that Sammy was pregnant, he would tell himself that at least it had been "a clean break".

When, straight after the big row, Sam asked Laszlo to spend a night sleeping on her couch, she meant only that she wanted company and support; but there was also the half-formed resolve that if her emotions and his should lead them on to something more (as they very nearly had once or twice in the past), she wouldn't resist. She would follow her feelings. That was what her head told her — that she should follow her heart. It was like a person lost in a snowstorm telling herself to follow another who was even more lost. It might lead somewhere, anywhere, nowhere.

The problem was that Laszlo would not take the lead. He seemed to have guessed that there was trouble between her and Freddy. He wanted to be helpful, and not a nuisance. She longed for him to be a nuisance but didn't know how to tell him. She wanted him to kiss her, touch her. Even a little force wouldn't have been unwelcome — anything that lifted from her the burden of responsibility for "what happened next" in the story of her life. But Laszlo did nothing — nothing except look too long at her and then look away, as if he couldn't believe what he thought he saw there. It was something her mother, the hated Marie, had told her once about men. When sensitivity was called for they were bullish; when a bit of bullishness mightn't go amiss, they tip-toed about and kept their voices down.

What made it worse during those few days after Christmas was that she and Laszlo had such a nice time together. It was so good to be with someone who wasn't always looking at his watch (Freddy used to look at his when they were wrapped around one another in bed, glancing at it over her shoulder and thinking she didn't notice); someone who didn't have a wife and child always on his mind; someone who wasn't always checking before he entered a café with her to be sure there was no one who might "report back".

Laszlo brought her breakfast in bed. He sang Shakespearean songs in the kitchen and danced with her, ballroom style, in the living room. He talked knowledgeably about her *Secret History of Modernism*. He told her about James I's book on witches, and how Shakespeare had written *Macbeth* to flatter the Scottish king. He explained how *Measure for Measure* could be read as a fierce attack on Puritans who wanted the theatres closed. He told her how *Coriolanus* had caused riots in Paris in the 1930s because Leftists thought its hero was a fascist and Rightists saw him as a noble warrior, the saviour of his nation. Laszlo offered these things not just as sets of facts but as stories. With Laszlo everything was a story. He was clever; and because she was too, cleverness was an aphrodisiac.

It was nice that he was kind, but Sam was longing for another kind of kindness. Pregnancy, she was finding, when it didn't make her sick made her sexy. Not for the first time, but for the first time seriously, comprehensively, she'd begun to imagine fucking Laszlo.

Then, interrupting it all, came How Repulsive and the telegram from Laszlo's dad. Of course he had to go and find out what it meant. But she was worried that nothing had been said; nothing between them had been brought out into the open. She tried to settle Laszlo down so they could talk, but he wouldn't be still, couldn't focus. This message from his father meant that something serious had happened at home. Somebody might be dying, or dead. Of course. She understood that. How could he think about anything else?

And then he really was going, and she panicked. Without warning, or without much warning, she kissed him. It was a full-on kiss, all open mouth and tongue and even teeth. He raced away, wiping his face with his open hand.

Sammy felt hot all over. It was as if her whole body was blushing. She'd been a fool, behaved like a woman on the rebound. Laszlo Winter didn't love her — not in that way.

Embarrassment made her angry. She hated Laszlo. He was detestable. It wouldn't have been so bad if he hadn't wiped his mouth. When she thought of that — his fright, his wild eyes, his hand wiping away her saliva — she wanted him up in that Russian rocket alongside Laica and Freddy Goldstein. The three of them, they could die together, sitting up. She wouldn't care. She imagined the rocket making a big white streak across the night sky as it burned up. She would watch it and rejoice.

That was what she thought, how she felt, what she told herself, recovering on her knees in the bathroom next morning, her mouth burning with vomit.

For two or three days Sammy avoided Laszlo — or perhaps (how could she be sure?) he was avoiding her. And then it was too late, he was gone. In the night she woke saying, "I want my mother." It was a shock. Her mother? How could this be? But it was true. It didn't change with morning. What she wanted was to be with Marie.

Telegrams were exchanged, toll calls were made. The mother made a booking to fly to London, then cancelled it and made a booking for the daughter to come to Sydney.

Before Laszlo got back to London Sam was doing what he had done, but around the other way, west to east – the Qantas 707 kangaroo-hop – London, Athens, Bahrain, Bombay, Singapore, Darwin, Sydney.

In the cool of the Beecroft verandah, looking out at the gum trees, hearing the raucous birds announcing themselves, Sammy discussed the pregnancy with Marie. Coolly, reasonably, they considered the options, and decided she would have the child, because the back-street alternative was too frightening, and because (mother and daughter agreed about this) her father, whatever she might want or he might think, wouldn't, couldn't, perform an abortion on his daughter – couldn't even be asked about it.

He could however, and did, deliver his grandchild, whom they named Leo because Leo was close to Laszlo and less foreign, and because by that time Sam had forgiven her friend who had wiped away her kiss, and was able to remember him with love and with regret. But the little boy would also be Israel – Leo Israel Conlan – in case in later years, when he asked who his father was and learned about his inheritance, he should decide that the Jew in him was the part he cared about most.

"But he never did," Sam concluded in one of her emails. "He knows about it, accepts it, but it's not important to him. He's always thought of my father as his dad. Takes after him. Has followed him into medicine. Leo's a surgeon, twice married already, father of two girls."

Sammy herself married only once – that was what she calls her "mistake with poor old Stiltzy". After that, she says, there was the social revolution of the late 1960s which "put an end to the need". "I've had a private life," she says, "but the roof over my head has been my own."

I take all of that in, think it admirable in its way, and wonder whether I would still like her. I don't intend to find out. Better to let her remain what she was, what she is, a star in my sky, a brilliant and beautiful young person with whom I was once in love.

But there was still that "small thing" I'd promised to do for her by way of recompense for these answers to my questions, this correcting of facts and filling of gaps. It was that I would see if I could discover what became of Freddy Goldstein after he returned to New Zealand; perhaps even find a way of meeting him.

I have Jewish friends in Auckland and put them on to the case. Within forty-eight hours they'd located him. A widower now, Freddy had moved to a retirement village in the Bay of Plenty. There had been only the one child, Meir. Ruth had been unable to have more. As a young adult Meir had gone to Israel and was now living there permanently, married with three children. Freddy was alone.

I drove down and called on him without preliminaries, without warning. I found him sitting on the minute patio, or forecourt, of his apartment, looking out over a lawn bordered with flax and cabbage trees, which sloped down to an arm of the Tauranga harbour. There was a pair of binoculars around his neck and a newspaper on the chair beside the one he was sitting in. Indoors, the radio was tuned to the Concert Programme.

I introduced myself only by saying I came with greetings from his friends Ben and Rachel in Auckland. He stood up, shook my hand, picked up the newspaper so I could take the second chair. We sat side by side looking at a scene composed almost entirely of greens and blues.

I said it was lovely and he agreed that it was. He hadn't begun to tire of it, and thought it would "see him out".

"I use these . . ." (he lifted the binoculars) "to watch the bird life down there. We get all kinds of waders. Grey herons, oystercatchers – and what I think are godwits. My neighbour tells me they migrate annually to Siberia. I'm going to get a book on it from the library."

He put the glasses to his eyes. After a moment he unhooked them from his neck and offered them to me. "Can you see that fellow down there?"

I looked where he pointed and focused on a grey heron wading in the shallows.

"He's hunting just now," Freddy said. "But when they take to the air – for elegance, they get the gold."

Up close I watched the grey, ruffle-winged bird on its stilts, its spear at the ready. It stopped, eyed the glassy water, stalked on. Suddenly it stabbed, had something that flashed a moment and was swallowed, shaken down the open throat. Soon the big bird was up and away, lazily over the water, the stilts tucked under and dragged behind.

"Beautiful," I said, handing back the glasses.

"I watch the golf course over there too. Don't know anything about golf, but one can watch in the spirit of anthropology. Golfers are a tribe. But it wouldn't do to approach too close." He chuckled at his own joke.

He put the strap back over his head and rested the glasses on his paunch. He was quite stout. His hair was white, his eyes blue, his face still handsome. I remembered Sammy saying he looked like Norman Mailer; that he was a Jew who could have passed himself off as a member of the SS.

He said, "But you didn't come to watch the birds, Mr . . ."

I told him to please call me Les. It was the name I'd taken for a time when I was a schoolboy and hadn't liked the foreignness of Laszlo. "I'm very happy to watch the birds," I told him. "But I looked in just, really, to ask whether you're well and happy. That's what your friends want to hear."

"Oh I'm well," he said. "Look at me." He thumped his chest.

I pressed him. "And happy?"

"Not *un*happy," he said.

I suppose I looked as if I wanted to hear more because he asked had I read Stephen Spender's journals, and when I said I hadn't he explained: "Someone asked Spender why he always seemed happy. He said because he didn't feel he had a right to be *un*happy. I understand that. I've known people who . . ." He hesitated. "Who *qualify*. I'm not one of them."

There was something immediate about Freddy Goldstein. He hardly looked at me, only glanced, but his voice was relaxed as if we knew one another. It made it easy to say, "I'm interested in your family story."

"Ah yes," he said. He must have assumed I'd heard it from his friends. "Well, it's just part of the bigger story. A small part."

He told me he'd long ago sent his son to Israel. "He went to be with his great-uncle Klaus. Klaus of course is long gone, but Meir's a pretty tough Zionist these days. Married with kids. He won't come back."

I asked what he thought of that.

He pulled a sad face. "It made Ruth unhappy to have him

leave us. Now she's gone and I don't have either of them. But Meir's there, he's alive . . ."

"And Israel?"

"Israel exists. Israel must survive."

I thought there was a hesitation and guessed it might not be unconnected with the news of the past few days. Fighting had broken out on the occupied West Bank, Israeli bullets against Arab stones. Dozens of young Arabs were dead, scores wounded. The Israeli occupying force was imposing curfews.

I was on the point of asking did he perhaps think it would have been better if Israel . . .

If Israel what, though? Dismantled settlements and withdrew from the occupied territories was probably what I had in mind. But how could I press present political problems on one who bore such a keen sense of their history?

So I didn't ask. But he must have known what was on my mind, and he found his own oblique way of answering the question that hadn't been asked.

"Let me tell you a story," he said. "I read it somewhere – in something in there." He waved towards a low table in his flat that was littered with books, magazines and overseas papers.

It was about an elderly Tel Aviv Jew who had been evicted in 1938 from his apartment in Vienna. He had managed to get out and away to Palestine, but all his books had been left behind, and that was the loss which troubled him most. It became the symbol, or the focus, of all the bad things that had happened to him. Years later, when the war was over, he revisited Vienna with his daughter. They stood in the courtyard looking up at where he had once lived. A woman, suspicious and unfriendly, asked what they wanted. He explained that he'd once lived there, and had left in a hurry.

"In 1938", he said, expecting she would know what that meant. All his books had been left behind. The woman, even more unfriendly, said there had been no books when she occupied the apartment after the war. That was all. He went back to Israel.

More years passed. The daughter lived with her husband in Jaffa in an apartment once occupied by Arabs, some of whom had been driven out by the 1948 Arab-Israeli War. One day she found two Arab women, mother and daughter, standing in the courtyard looking up at the windows of her apartment. She went and spoke to them. The mother had grown up there. The Jewish woman invited them in. They went through, looking at all the rooms, saying nothing, until suddenly the older woman asked, "Where are my father's books?"

"These are stories that cut deep for me," Freddy said. And a little later, as we sat in silence looking at the view: "Most of my dreams these days are of Berlin. My first home." He smiled. "I had a very nice train set that got left behind."

I wondered whether that had been before his first departure, or after the return, but didn't want to alarm him by revealing too suddenly how well I knew his story.

"I try not to think too much about these things," he said. "I mean about rights and wrongs. They can keep you awake at night, and nothing changes. Better to dream than to think."

He had no German accent, but no New Zealand accent either. It was strange, a rather formal English, but neutral, belonging nowhere. I said, "I knew someone long ago who told me you had a shadowy first language in your head that you couldn't quite get at or use. It was there but out of reach."

He was smiling, surprised, interested. "There are several languages," he confirmed. "Bits of Yiddish. Quite a lot of

Hebrew. But mostly my infant German. I still have some songs, and some rhymes. Words and phrases. But my father wouldn't have it spoken in the house, so I lost it. It's gone, but it's there. I sometimes think if I got a serious blow to the head I might wake up speaking German."

He asked who it was had told me about his sense of a lost language. I said it was Samantha Conlan.

Now he looked at me more carefully. "Of course, of course. I've seen your photograph in the papers. You're Laszlo Winter. I'm sorry. I should have recognized you."

The talk was more direct now, franker – mostly about Sam. We put our knowledge and our memories together.

"So you fell in love with her," he said. "And then?"

"And then she became pregnant. But not to me."

Now there was a longer silence. "Are you here to tell me something?" he asked at last.

"Only if you feel you'd like to know."

He pondered before he said, "I heard about the birth of her child. I knew it couldn't be mine – or I thought I knew . . ."

Much later, after a great deal more talk and a pot of coffee indoors, he said as I was leaving, "So I am grandfather of five. I thought it was only three."

"And the father of an Australian surgeon."

He smiled and shook my hand. "Tell them I'm here if it's of any interest. If it's not, they can count on my absence and my silence. I wish them well. I send them my love."

As I was driving back to Auckland I remembered something else he'd said: "I tell myself I have only two duties. Not to forget my history altogether. And to love the human race." And then he'd smiled, almost laughed at himself. "Impossible, of course, but it's the thought that counts."

SEVENTEEN

The Secret History of Modernism

THE SKY IS BLUE AND HIGH AND WIDE. THE PLUM IS IN full leaf, and the pear is in blossom with its white flowers that look as if they've been lightly sprinkled with pepper. The Hauraki Gulf stretches away, blue and glittering, measuring distance. Waiheke Island and Brown's Island lie low. Rangitoto lifts itself to its full height, dark, dormant, dominant, and promising nothing.

I have sent Sammy my report on Freddy Goldstein and she has thanked me for it. "I'm so glad you found him," she wrote, "and that you found him good company and intelligent. As I remember him – fondly – he was very bright, very articulate, very loveable, and very married."

A few days ago I sent her "my last email". I told her it was my last, that I wouldn't pester her any further, and I meant it. From where I sit, at home in St Heliers, Auckland, New Zealand, Sammy is a story, or a chapter of a story, that should be brought to a close. But there was one last thing that still nagged at me. I reminded her that she had once promised, if her *Secret History of Modernism* ever reached anything like a theory, or managed to explain itself, she would tell me its conclusions. So now I asked: was that point ever reached?

A day or so later her reply came. "My last to your last," she called it. And then, "What are we, Laszlo? Shoemakers?"

But she took my question seriously. It had forced her to do a proper hunt for her notebooks and typescripts. "I've found them," she wrote, "found more of them, and found them more interesting, than I expected."

And yes, I was right, there had been a theory forming before she gave it up. "Freddy had challenged me to explain why all the great Modernist writers of that period had been fascists. It wasn't true, of course, but nearly true. True enough to make you wonder."

She went on, "I decided it had something to do with tossing out the nineteenth century Romantic idea of beauty – dismissing it as soft and sentimental. The new art and literature would (who was it said this?) 'burn with a hard, gem-like flame'. The new blade would cut through the butter of the past. There would be a new discipline in writing and in thought, and also in social and political life. It was going to be all steel and sinew and will. Like most *avant garde* ideas this had its own logic and its own truth. But undiluted, it was a poison.

"But when I look at my final notes I can see where this line of thought ran into the sand. At first I tried to argue that the Hitler rallies were really works of Modernist art. But then when I tried to connect them – as art – with what followed, right down to the camps, the lethal 'showers', the 'ovens' that were crematoria, the whole exercise started to seem frivolous. I kept coming back guiltily to the thought of poor Freddy with his anxieties, his dark dreams, his lost language and culture, his persecuted and murdered family. Theory seemed a poor sort of urn for the ashes, and I gave up."

Later in the same message she wrote, "I think now that my

Secret History of Modernism was really the secret history of my love of Freddy. You put an end to that, Laszlo, so you put an end to them both."

And now my memoir is finished. Louise has been reading it. Over breakfast she says, "You are very historical, *mon cher*. And whimsical I think."

I find this, like many of her remarks, opaque, even mysterious; and I know that to enquire further would only deepen the mystery. So I say, dismissively, but also sincerely, "Of course it's too literary. I know that."

"No no, Laszlo." Louise doesn't accept this. "Not at all." She tells me, "The novel I'm reading – by Moravia – in the chapter I read last night he refers to Proust, and then . . . Wait."

She goes into the next room and comes back with a paperback, *L'uomo que guarda*. "Here it is. He names two characters from Proust. Then Herodutus. Then he quotes a whole poem of Mallarmé's and analyses it. A little further on . . ." She turns pages, hunting. "Here it is. Baudelaire. He quotes a line of Baudelaire's. Then there's something about Hamlet and Polo . . ."

"Polonius?"

"Polonius. And then towards the end there's something about paintings by Manet and Titian."

I ask does anything happen in this chapter. She tells me a lot happens. The narrator meets a black woman in Rome and she lets him photograph her, naked.

"Yes, well, of course . . ." I say, not saying anything. "But just the same . . ."

"Just the same what, *mon Oncle?*"

"Just the same Moravia's Italian. And you, my darling, are French. And I, unfortunately, am – well you know what I am and who I'm writing for. There's a difference."

"*A bas la différence*," she says.

That was this morning. I've spent the day ambling on the beaches and on the rocks between the bays, and reading in the seafront cafés. It's good to have had Louise's support for what I've written; but despite her defence, I know that when she's done with it I will read it over myself and then it must go away into the metal trunk where all my rejects are stored and forgotten. It could never be published, not while this person and that person is still, or may still be, alive, here or there or somewhere else, ready to take offence and just a phone call away from a lawyer. Some time ago I told Sammy I was writing fiction but it wasn't true then and it hasn't become true since. In its way the memoir is my own *Secret History of Modernism*. Like hers, it will never see the light of day.

So what now?

I have no choice. Those dreams of bike-riding, weight-lifting, house-building, living out a half-life in movie houses, or dying the slow glorious death of French food and wine – they were not entirely serious; could not have been if I had given any thought at all to our bank balance. Writer's block is an idea I can no longer entertain, a luxury I can not at present afford.

Fiction calls.

Fiction about what, though? I don't know yet, do I? – not until I make a start. But there has been an idea forming, half an idea . . . A faint pricking of the thumbs . . . Something about Australian Sammy and New Zealand-Jewish Freddy and the dark history Freddy brought with him; about Rajiv and the old Empire and the *deeps* of the Indian mind; about Margot and Mark and Siegmund and Sieglinde; about Oxford and the Wind in the Willows; about "robust" Heather and Shakespeare and "the shop" . . .

All of that, and more — and myself somewhere in there, knocking blindly about among them in that far-distant past that was London before the sixties, when "You've never had it so good" made a kind of sense.

Yes, it's possible. Something might come of it. I will begin in the morning.

ACKNOWLEDGEMENTS

The author and publisher gratefully acknowledge the permission to reprint extracts from the poems of W. B. Yeats, from *The Collected Poems of W. B. Yeats* (Macmillan, 1966) by permission of A. P. Watt Ltd on behalf of Michael B. Yeats; and T. S. Eliot, from *Collected Poems* 1909–62 (Faber & Faber, 1974) by permission of Faber & Faber.

350 gen 01.0517 on